His offer was too good to be true...

"I'm suggesting we marry," Drogo coolly announced to Annis. "That way we can each do what's supposed to be impossible—have our cake and eat it."

Annis sat staring at him in transfixed disbelief until Drogo broke the silence.

"You think I'm not serious?" he murmured. "Because I am. Never more so."

"How can you be?" she expostulated. "Why, we scarcely know each other!"

"You and I know all that's necessary," he said smoothly.

"And love," Annis prodded, "is that unimportant?"

"Don't you feel you could be happy as my wife?" He leaned toward her, his strange tawny eyes holding her gaze, so that she found it impossible to look away. "You didn't appear to find my kisses unpleasant before you felt bound to resist them."

ANNE WEALE
is also the author of these
Harlequin Romances

and these

Harlequin Presents

Bed of Roses

by

ANNE WEALE

Harlequin Books

TORONTO • LONDON • LOS ANGELES • AMSTERDAM
SYDNEY • HAMBURG • PARIS • STOCKHOLM • ATHENS • TOKYO

Original hardcover edition published in 1981
by Mills & Boon Limited

ISBN 0-373-02484-3

Harlequin edition published June 1982

CHAPTER ONE

THE first time she felt his presence was when, having been asleep on her woven grass beach mat, she woke up and stretched like a cat. Her bare golden-brown, rose-tipped breasts bobbing as she sprang to her feet, she strolled lazily down the white beach to the placid lagoon to refresh her warm skin in the water.

It was not her habit to sleep through the hot afternoons, but the day before had been Book Day—the day, once a month, when a boat delivered their mail and supplies, including a parcel of books—and she had been reading most of the night.

Silvanus did much of his work at night, and never slept for more than four hours. But Annis, being over half a century younger, and full of the physical energy of her nineteen years, needed eight hours' sleep, sometimes more.

It was partly because the sun was in her eyes, and partly because she was still drowsy, that she did not notice immediately the yacht which had anchored outside the reef while she had been lying on her mat.

But for a sudden glint of brightness she might not have noticed it at all, as she waded into the lagoon. Perhaps the vessel had swung slightly on her moorings, causing a metal fitting to flash in the brilliant sunlight. Whatever the cause, the sparkle caught Annis's attention and made her pause, thigh-deep in water, her hands going up to her forehead to make a shade for her eyes.

It was then, as she stood there, naked, that she saw a tall man on the deck looking at her through his field-glasses.

That it was she at whom he was looking, and not something in the tangle of undergrowth behind her, was confirmed when he lowered the glasses and waved to her.

Almost, she returned the gesture. She was so used to going bare-skinned about the beaches that she was seldom conscious of her nakedness, and most of the shipping she saw was too far away to cause her any selfconsciousness.

But where she was standing the lagoon was narrow, and the yacht was not more than a few hundred yards offshore. His field-glasses would give him a much closer view of her uncovered body than she wished to allow to a stranger.

Her impression of him, in the seconds before she plunged out of sight, was of black hair and darkly-bronzed skin. Then the heat and the air were cut off as she dived below the surface into the cool, dim privacy of her other element, the sea.

Born and reared on a privately-owned island, remote from the gay resorts of the tourist parts of the Caribbean, Annis had learned to swim before she could walk. Although lacking the heavy shoulders and muscular arms of many competitive women swimmers, she could have outswum most of them, both on and under the water. Swimming was her principal exercise. The island afforded limited walking; and a lifetime of daily swimming had given her speed and stamina on the surface, and an ability to stay underneath it for far longer than most people could.

If the man on the yacht was still watching for her, which possibly he wasn't, all he would see was occasional glimpses of her seal-sleek head as she surfaced to refill her lungs before disappearing again until she had reached the next beach and was hidden from his view by the spit of sand with a group of palm trees growing on it.

When she returned to the house, Silvanus was at work in his study. She knew this because the door was closed: a warning to her not to disturb him.

For most of his life—he was now in his middle seventies —he had been a distinguished biographer, much praised by the literary critics, but unknown to the general public because none of his subjects had had the perennial appeal of Mary Queen of Scots, Napoleon, Queen Victoria, Lord Byron and other eternally charismatic figures.

Since his retirement to the island, his work had changed course. For the past fifteen years he had been engaged upon a voluminous retelling of the myths of ancient Greece.

Annis had not always lived alone with him. Until she was twelve, her mother had been with them; a woman as scholarly as Sylvanus, yet with a domesticated side, and also a lively sense of humour. Had Mary Rossiter lived, it had been her intention to send her daughter to England, to the famous boarding school from which she herself had gone on to excel at university.

But Mary had died as Annis entered her teens, and Sylvanus had not wished to part with the child. He had told himself, and told her, that the world had little to offer her. The truth was that he was too old for the world and well content with his hideaway.

Loving him, and loving the island, Annis had been equally content to replace her mother as his companion and housekeeper. The world would not run away. It would still be there when Sylvanus had gone. She could wait.

By the time he emerged from his study, a rich fish stew was simmering, awaiting his pleasure, and Annis was rocking gently in the hammock slung on the verandah, re-

reading verses called *Sea Love* in an anthology which had
come with the new books.

> *Tide be runnin' the great world over:*
> *'Twas only last June month I mind that we*
> *Was thinkin' the toss and the call in the breast of*
>   *the lover*
> *So everlastin' as the sea.*
>
> *Here's the same little fishes that sputter and swim,*
> *Wi' the moon's old glim on the grey, wet sand;*
> *An' him no more to me nor me to him*
> *Than the wind goin' over my hand.*

'Did Harriet ever know a poet called Charlotte Mew who
lived from 1869 to 1928?' she asked Sylvanus, when he
joined her on the fly-screened verandah where they sat after
dark to avoid being disturbed by insects attracted by the
lamplight.

'Mew ... Charlotte Mew ...' Sylvanus searched the re-
cesses of his phenomenal memory. Harriet, the wife of his
youth, had been a fellow biographer, much in the literary
swim of her day. 'Ah, yes, I thought the name had a
familiar ring. She was the odd little woman whose sister
restored some antique furniture for us.'

'Why was she odd?' asked Annis, tipping herself out of
the hammock in which, after they had eaten, he would re-
cline, reading and sipping a large tot of rum.

'Tiny little creature, less than five feet tall, with a mop of
grey hair. Took her own life.'

'Oh, poor thing! Do you know why?'

'Unbalanced by grief for her sister, so it was said. There
was some madness in the family, which was why they—

the two eldest girls—had made a pact never to marry.'

This sad background to the disillusioned poem kept Annis pityingly silent while she laid the table and dished up the supper.

More often than not Sylvanus would eat his meals with a book propped in front of him. Sometimes whole days would pass with scarcely a word exchanged between them. Tonight, however, the old man was in the mood to discuss his day's work with her. He would gossip about the ancient Greeks, real and legendary, as if they were people he had known before becoming a recluse.

Once a year, to honour his promise to her mother, he would break his seclusion to take Annis to an island where she could have her teeth checked and—when she was younger—replace her outgrown garments. Not that she needed much clothing, and her shoes, all her life, had been cheap pairs of white canvas plimsolls which she wore only when her feet needed some protection from coral and the spines of sea urchins.

Supper was over, and he had settled in the hammock while she dealt with the dishes which had to be washed straight away or they would attract trains of ants, when she heard him call her.

'What's the matter?' she asked, judging by his tone that something was amiss.

'We have a visitor. Fetch my revolver, would you, please?'

The house was built on the highest point of the island to catch every breath of wind and to have sea views on all sides, although parts of the shoreline were hidden from sight by wooded areas.

Looking down in the direction of the beach where she had had her afternoon nap, Annis saw that, with the aid of a torch, someone—perhaps more than one person—was coming up the track.

She fetched from a drawer in his bedroom the firearm which he kept there, loaded, as a precaution against intruders who, having heard that an old man and a young girl lived on their own there, might think, erroneously, there were money and valuables to be had for the taking. In fact there was neither, and not much money in the bank. All Sylvanus's books were long out of print, and their only income came from the royalties on a history book for schools written by Mary Rossiter.

'There was a yacht lying off Big Beach earlier. She must still be there,' said Annis, when she brought the gun to him, holding it gingerly because she was frightened of it.

Sylvanus took it in his right hand, the book in his left concealing the weapon from whoever was approaching the house. To the ever-present chirping of the male cicadas in the undergrowth now was added the clear, flute-like notes of a man whistling what Annis recognised as a snatch from Vivaldi's *Four Seasons*.

'He announces himself—a point in his favour,' murmured Sylvanus.

The man who, a little later, entered the circle of light cast by the oil lamps was immediately recognisable to Annis as the one who had waved to her.

He was very tall, several inches over six feet, and built in splendid proportion to his great height. At the distance from which she had seen him before, he could have belonged to one of the dark-skinned racial groups in the Caribbean. But now, at closer quarters, she could see that he was of European stock with a swarthier than average skin which had taken on its gypsy-darkness through being constantly exposed to the sun.

He was wearing a bright yellow shirt tucked inside a pair of white trousers with loops at the waist through which a black belt was slotted. The ends of a colourful scarf were pulled through a ring at the base of his strong brown neck.

'Good evening,' he said, with a somewhat un-English bow, although his voice sounded English. 'I am Drogo Wolfe. I hope this is not an inconvenient time to call on you, Mr Rossiter. I have a request to make, sir.'

The old-fashioned courtesy of the 'sir' was just what Sylvanus liked and found increasingly lacking in the modern world, whenever he returned to it. Yet it flashed through Annis's mind that Drogo Wolfe looked as if it were usually he who was called sir. There was something about him which even she, cut off from life as she was, recognised as the power to command other men.

'Let Mr Wolfe in,' said Sylvanus and, when she had opened the screen door, 'This is my daughter, Annis.'

Such few strangers as they encountered usually took her to be his granddaughter, and were often visibly astonished that a man of his age should have a daughter of hers.

If Drogo Wolfe was surprised, he did not reveal it. 'How do you do, Miss Rossiter?' he said, offering his hand as if this was the first time he had set eyes on her.

'How do you do?'

She felt her hand firmly enclosed in the controlled grip of a man whose muscular wrists and long brown fingers could, had he not been careful, have exerted a painful force on the hand of a woman or a man of lesser physique.

He turned to shake hands with her father, raising an eyebrow in slight surprise when Sylvanus put the gun aside on a table within reach of his hand.

'A wise precaution, I daresay, when you have only yourselves to rely on,' said their visitor dryly.

'How is it that you know our name, Mr Wolfe?' asked her father, as he gestured for him to be seated.

'It was told me by the skipper of the yacht I've chartered. He seems to know a great deal about this part of the Caribbean, but had he not known that this island was in private hands, and the owner's name was Rossiter, I should have recognised you.'

'Recognised me? Have we met before? I don't recall it.'

'There must be a great many people who, never having met you, would recognise you, sir. Although it was taken twenty years ago, you are still very like the photograph which appeared on the jacket of your life of Garibaldi.'

'You've read it, have you? When did you come across it? At the time it came out you must have been still a schoolboy.'

Evidently her father judged him, as she did, to be somewhere in his early thirties.

'Yes, that is so,' he agreed. 'I read it a few years ago, on a flight from London to New York before Concorde speeded up the journey.'

'Concorde?' The name meant nothing to the Rossiters.

'A supersonic airliner made jointly by the French and the British which can fly at up to one thousand, three hundred and fifty miles an hour, thereby reducing the transatlantic flight to three and a half hours. By local time, Concorde arrives at New York earlier than it leaves London.'

'Good God! What will be the next folly? How does it benefit mankind to achieve these unnecessary speeds?' was Sylvanus's irritable reaction.

'It benefits those employed on the project, and those who found the subsonic flight a waste of a day,' the younger man replied mildly.

Suddenly Annis had a strong intuition that, in spite of

his outward deference, privately he thought her father a
foolish old josser with whom he would not waste his time
were it not to his own advantage.

She surprised herself, and both men, by saying abruptly,
'You mentioned a request, Mr Wolfe. What kind of request?'

He turned to where she was standing and his eyes, a
strange dark hazel colour, travelled from her face to her
feet. She was wearing a white cotton blouse and a blue
skirt, several years old and a darker colour below the line
of the original hem. But she felt he was seeing not her
clothes but the body beneath them; her brown and pink
breasts, the small volution of her navel in the swell of her
stomach, and the triangle of curly hair at the apex of her
thighs. He had seen her in intimate detail, and the gleam
in his eyes suggested that he was remembering every line
and curve of her.

A bright blush suffused her cheeks which her father took
for confusion of another sort.

He said, on a note of reproof, 'Mr Wolfe may like some
refreshment, Annis.'

'Thank you—no. I don't want to intrude for any longer
than I must. My request is simple. I came to ask if you
would allow me and my guests to land on one of your
beaches for our lunch tomorrow. Naturally you have my
assurance that we shall not leave behind any sign of our
presence.'

'You are welcome, my dear sir—most welcome,' Sylvanus
replied, his mood unwontedly hospitable. 'How many
guests have you with you?'

'We're a party of six. Perhaps you and your daughter
would care to join us?'

'It's kind of you, but I think not. We are not gregarious,' said her father.

'Then I'll say goodnight.' Drogo Wolfe rose to his full height, and gave his un-English bow.

As she opened the screen door for him, Annis avoided his eyes.

'Goodnight, Miss Rossiter.'

'Goodnight.' Her cheeks were still warm from the fiery colour he had raised in them moments ago.

He stepped quickly out through the door to avoid letting insects fly in but, as she closed it behind him, he paused to say, 'Which beach would you recommend for our picnic? We don't want to drive you away from your own preferred bathing place.'

'Any of the leeward bays would suit you. I'll swim on the windward side tomorrow. I like all our beaches,' she answered.

'Very well. Thank you.' He turned away.

From behind, his shoulders looked even wider and more powerful than they did from the front. His broad back tapered to hips as lean as those of a youth of Annis's age. His whole body had the appearance of being in vigorous use; he had none of the flaccid spare flesh of most of the tourists she had seen on her trips to the dentist.

When he had disappeared into the darkness and was out of earshot, her father said, 'I considered it somewhat out of place for you to demand of our visitor the reason for his call, my child. That was for me to enquire.'

'Yes, I'm sorry, Father,' she answered. 'I—I don't know why, I didn't take to him.'

'Indeed? I thought him a very civil sort of fellow. For what reason did you dislike him?'

'No reason ... just instinct.'

Sylvanus, quoting a remark by Lucetta in Shakespeare's play *The Two Gentlemen of Verona*, said, ' "I have no other but a woman's reason; I think him so because I think him so".'

This, accompanied by a smile, indicated that she was forgiven for her misdeed and, having returned the revolver to the drawer, Annis went back to the kitchen to finish her tasks there.

That night, when she went to her room, before she climbed into bed and adjusted the tent of fine white netting suspended by a hook from a rafter, she spent some time staring at her reflection in the misty old glass of the eighteenth-century dressing mirror which her mother had brought out from England.

Mary Rossiter's grandmother had been a Scandinavian, and it was from this Norwegian great-grandmother that Annis must have inherited her naturally ash-blonde hair. She had never had it cut, and it hung down her back almost to the base of her spine: a thick skein of silver-gilt silk.

Her eyes, thickly and darkly lashed, were grey. The natural colour of her skin was unknown to her. It might be white, it might be creamy. For the present it was everywhere brown except on the palms of her hands and the soles of her feet. Nor could she be sure of being pretty. On the last two trips to the dentist she had been aware of men's eyes on her, but that might only have been because she was her father's daughter, and people always stared at Sylvanus. Even those who didn't know him to be the eccentric owner of Morne Island were struck by his massive bulk and Bohemian style of dress, although this was less striking now than it had been when Annis was a child. Nowadays the tourists and residents of the town island were themselves less conventional in their dress, and sometimes she and Sylvanus were hard put to it not to stare at scantily-clad vacationers turning as pink as cooked lobsters and exposing bulges much better concealed from the public eye.

In spite of her instinctive mistrust of the man, she could not help regretting that her father had declined Mr Wolfe's invitation to join the lunch party. Probably the food would be delicious. Although she did her best with home-grown produce, fresh fish, and the canned and dried foods brought by the supply boat, inevitably their diet was lacking in the variety available to people living on the large and populous islands.

She fell asleep thinking of pistachio ice cream, which she had not tasted for six months, and would not taste again for another six months.

Annis had never possessed a watch. Her father's old-fashioned gold hunter lay unused in the drawer with the revolver. They had a clock but never wound it, and had they wished to keep it going they had no radio by which to check its accuracy. The Rossiters lived by sun-time; judging the hour by the angle of the light and the length of certain shadows.

Annis always woke at first light and by sunrise was eating her breakfast. After that her first task of the day was to do some work on her vegetable patch. Later she would sweep through the house with a grass broom before dealing with one of the bookshelves. On the island books were endangered by humidity and by insects. In a house lined with books it was necessary to keep a systematic check on their condition. Washing clothes was a minor chore, and ironing them even less onerous. Thus most of her time was her own although, brought up by two scholars, she would have felt any day in which she had taught herself nothing to have been a day wasted.

Sylvanus had ceased to supervise her education on her seventeenth birthday, a little more than two years ago. Since then she had devised and followed a programme of her own. Like her mother before her, she was deeply interested in history.

On the day of Drogo Wolfe's beach party, she intended, as she had told him, to keep to the windward side of the island. But all morning she felt curiosity fermenting inside her until she knew there was no way she could contain it. It was not that she wished to see him again, she told herself. His guests were the lure which drew her to whichever of the leeward bays had been chosen for the picnic.

All the bays had paths leading to them, kept open by Annis hacking back, with a machete, the encroachments of ferns and vines which would, had the paths been neglected, very soon have obliterated them.

When the sound of voices and laughter led her to a concealed vantage point overlooking the venue of the picnic, she saw that all but two people were disporting themselves in the lagoon. The two ashore were undoubtedly the charter skipper and his wife. They were busy setting up a barbecue. An awning to throw a patch of shade on the dazzling whiteness of the sand had already been rigged, and deck-chairs and air-beds brought ashore from the yacht which, having brought her father's telescope with her, she could see now had the name *Sunseeker* painted on her white bows.

Not altogether easy in her mind about the ethics of watching people unbeknown to them, but as fascinated by them as they probably were by the brightly-coloured fish which inhabited the coral gardens, Annis turned her attention to the people in the water.

Three male heads and three female heads suggested three married couples. She wondered which of the women was Drogo's wife, and what she would have thought had she come on deck yesterday to find him studying a naked girl through his field-glasses.

When the bathers emerged from the water, one couple were hand in hand, and the third man and one of the women were at least ten years older than Drogo Wolfe. So the one in the gold bikini must be Mrs Wolfe. She looked about twenty-five, with dark hair and large dark brown eyes. Having blotted herself lightly with a towel, she re-painted her lips a glossy dark red and then placed a cigarette between them. It was lit for her by the older man. Drogo had strolled across to the barbecue. Clad only in brief saffron trunks, his tanned skin glistening with droplets, he looked like an ancient Greek athlete; his thick wet black hair curling against the nape of his sinewy neck and sending a trickle of water down the centre of his back where every movement of his arms caused a ripple of muscle.

Presently he returned to the others who were being served with pale golden wine in tall conical glasses by the skipper while his wife began to barbecue chops. After watching the way she did this for some minutes, Annis looked back at the others to find Drogo was no longer with them. Assuming he had retired out of sight for only a few minutes, she thought no more about it until his voice, saying quietly from behind her, 'I had a feeling you might be more gregarious than your father, Miss Rossiter,' made her gasp and whirl round to find him watching her with an unconcealed glint of amusement.

'M—Mr Wolfe!' she stammered, deeply embarrassed. 'H-how did you know I was here?'

'The psychology of your sex is not a closed book to me

as it seems to be to some men,' he answered. 'You're how old?'

His unusually dark hazel eyes repeated the appraisal of her body which had made her blush the night before: and today she was wearing only a faded turquoise bikini which, bought when she was sixteen, was now really one size too small for her.

'Seventeen? Eighteen?' he estimated.

'I'm nineteen.' Again rich colour suffused her honey-brown cheeks as his glance lingered on the curves of her breasts and hips.

'Only just nineteen, I should imagine.'

'Nineteen and two months.'

'Even so it's remarkable.'

'What is remarkable?'

'That you should be content to be kept here or, if not content, resigned to it. I could see in your face when last night I asked you to join us that *you* would have liked to accept the invitation. It followed that if you were not allowed to join us, you would probably watch our activities.'

'I wasn't "not allowed" to join. I didn't wish to,' she retorted, resenting his percipience.

'Then why are you here—like a child with its nose pressed against the window of the sweet-shop, looking longingly at the goodies inside?'

He grinned, and held out his hand to her. 'Come: my friends will feel themselves unwelcome if I tell them the owner's daughter refused to meet them.'

Annis stayed where she was, resisting the enticement of his outstretched hand.

He said, 'When I first saw you lying on the beach yesterday, with your head to the sea and your long hair spread on the sand, I thought you were a stranded mermaid. Until you lifted two legs instead of a tail.'

Her cheeks, which had cooled, grew hot again. It was something to be thankful for that she had been sleeping with her head towards the reef, and not the other way round. Even so, she found it acutely mortifying to recall being spreadeagled on the sand while he studied her through his glasses.

As if he could read her thoughts, he said, 'I think perhaps you don't realise that in Europe now it's quite usual for girls to bathe in the nude on certain beaches. And all the Mediterranean beaches are littered with topless sunbathers —some of whom would look better covered up,' he added sardonically.

'Really?' she said, in astonishment. Sylvanus was inclined to disapprove of the brevity of bikinis.

'Really,' he assured her. 'Now come and say hello to my friends, and have your first glass of champagne and some of the excellent smoked salmon with which we're starting our picnic.'

She could have resisted his magnetism—or so she told herself afterwards—but the temptation of champagne and smoked salmon was irresistible.

'Or perhaps, for a sea-nymph, caviar would be more appropriate,' he added reflectively. 'Do you know what caviar is?'

'Sturgeon's roe: the sturgeon being a large fish, sometimes twenty feet long, whose roe is made into caviar and the air-bladder into isinglass.'

'You've had caviar before?' he asked, on a note of surprise.

'No, never. I read about it in the dictionary. When I was fifteen, Father made me read four pages of the dictionary every day for a year. And our library includes most of the classics on food—Larousse, Brillat-Savarin, Escoffier. It's not a subject which interests my father much, but it did interest Mother.'

'Your mother is no longer here?'

'She died six years ago.'

'*Drogo! Where have you got to?*' came a shout from the beach.

'Coming!' he answered, and grasped her arm to steer her ahead of him.

Unaccustomed to meeting anyone but the skipper and crew of their supply boat, her dentist and one or two shopkeepers, Annis found it a daunting ordeal to be introduced to seven strangers.

'This is Annis Rossiter whose father owns Morne Island,' he told them, as the two men who had been seated rose to their feet at her approach.

The cynosure of six pairs of curious eyes, and one pair of unfriendly dark ones, she listened while he told her their names, but the only one which she registered was that of Nanette, in the gold bikini, who she sensed thought she was an interloper.

Both the other women seemed to realise she was shy, and were at pains to make her welcome.

'Bob, would you mind fetching some caviar,' Drogo said to the skipper.

'Oh, please—not especially for me,' Annis protested, in confusion.

'Why not? It won't take Bob a moment, and we have plenty of it on board. I never travel without it.'

'Have you never tried caviar, Annis?' the older woman asked her pleasantly. 'It's rather an acquired taste, Drogo. Not everyone shares your passion for it.'

'I don't for one,' said Nanette, her mouth turning down in distaste. 'To wake up and eat it at two in the morning as you do, Drogo—ugh, I don't know how you can!'

'We all have our idiosyncrasies. I don't share your pleasure in those things'—with a gesture at the cigarette dangling between her scarlet-tipped fingers.

His tone was mild, and yet for an instant his eyes had a hard, cold light as if her remark had displeased him.

For Annis it had confirmed that Nanette was his wife. When he had not introduced her as such, she had wondered if she might have been wrong about that. But although she was not so naïve as to be unaware of other relationships between men and women, it seemed unlikely that Nanette would have referred to his nocturnal habits unless they were husband and wife.

By this time the skipper had launched the dinghy and was rowing in the direction of the yacht, and his wife had left the barbecue and was offering a platter of smoked salmon garnished with thinly sliced cucumber and accompanied by rolled slices of brown bread and butter.

Everyone else already had a napkin, a plate, and a fork, and Drogo gave those which must have been meant for his use to Annis. This time she did not protest, having reached the conclusion that it was better to accept his arrangements without argument. A few moments later he gave her a glass of the gently bubbling golden wine which she knew now to be champagne.

Before the skipper returned she had grasped, from the conversation, that the older couple were David and Diana, and the other man, Mark, was Diana's brother. He was clearly in love with the girl called Susie. His eyes seldom left her. She, it seemed, was related to Drogo in some way.

'So you never go back to England to see your relations

or anything?' Susie said presently, having elicited the basic facts of Annis's life history. 'Are you happy here? Don't you want to explore the wider world?'

'Yes, and I expect I shall one day. But my father prefers to stay here, and I couldn't desert him. He was over fifty when he married my mother, his second wife. He's in his seventies now. It wouldn't be fair to leave him alone.'

'Aren't you ever lonely?' asked Susie. 'For people of your own age?'

'A little, sometimes. Not often. I imagine there are thousands of people doing dull, tiring jobs in big cities, who would envy me my life.'

'Millions, I should think,' was Mark's comment.

It was not long before Bob rowed back to the beach. He brought with him an earthenware jar, some black bread wrapped in a napkin, and a box containing sliced lemon.

'The Russians call caviar *Ikra*, and the choicest comes fresh from the sterlet, the small fish,' Drogo explained, as he opened the jar and showed her its contents, a mass of glistening, translucent grey globules. 'You must never let it come into contact with metal, and although it's sometimes served with finely minced onion and minced egg whites and yolks, I prefer it with lemon and parsley.'

Using a plastic spoon, he put some caviar on a piece of the black bread and offered it to her. To her renewed embarrassment, everyone watched her taste it.

She had thought the eggs would taste fishy, but in fact the flavour of the grains was unlike anything she had ever eaten before, and it was with spontaneous pleasure that, having swallowed them, she said, 'Oh, but it's *delicious*, isn't it?'

And then encountered a virulent glance from Nanette

which made her wish she had held her tongue, or at least modified her enjoyment.

David then made matters worse by giving a shout of laughter, and declaring, 'A girl after Drogo's own heart,' a remark which caused his wife and Susie to flicker glances at Nanette and then at each other in a way which Annis could not interpret.

Drogo himself seemed oblivious of the undercurrents which she could sense. He helped her to some more caviar, and heaped several spoonfuls on the black bread for himself.

'Excellent brain food,' he said. 'Do you have any form of cold storage up at the house?'

She shook her head.

'Pity. I would have given you a pot to eat at your leisure, but caviar spoils very quickly at any temperature above forty degrees.'

'No cold storage at all?' asked the skipper's wife. 'But, my dear, how do you manage?'

'As people managed before cold storage was invented, I suppose,' answered Annis lightly.

'Surely in this climate not to have cold drinks, or a place to keep perishable foodstuffs, must be rather trying, isn't it?' This comment was made by Diana.

'Not really. It's what I'm used to.' But Annis was suddenly conscious that although officially she was of the same nationality as these people and spoke the same language, in all other ways there was a great gulf between herself and them.

'And you would survive in a world without any more oil; whereas we, when the power peters out, will be lost without all our gadgets,' Drogo said drily.

She turned startled eyes to his face. 'Is the power going to peter out?'

'Our present sources of it must do so, but by that time there will be other ways to keep alive the machines which keep us alive.'

This remark led the men into a discussion of the alternative sources of power. Annis listened attentively, but the subject seemed to bore the other women, who soon launched a separate conversation about clothes.

After the barbecued chops, with which were served baked potatoes and a green salad, there were refreshing lemon sorbets before the cheese. This last course was refused by all the women except Annis to whom, as she had never read a woman's magazine, a calorie had to do with physics and not figures. Encouraged by Drogo, she sampled all the three cheeses, which were Brie, Roquefort and a strong farmhouse Cheddar.

'It's a pleasant change to see a girl eating heartily instead of starving herself,' he said when, after a second helping of Roquefort, she refused his offer to cut some more Brie for her.

'You would be the first to criticise if we all let ourselves go,' Nanette remarked rather acidly, her glance at the younger girl making Annis wonder if, by their standards, she was too plump.

Diana's figure was well rounded, but she was approaching middle age. Susie and Nanette were thin with small breasts, making her feel her own curves might be over-generous. Yet she hadn't read any criticism in Drogo's eyes when he had been appraising her earlier.

'More exercise is a better régime than less food. Most women don't take enough,' he said.

'How do you exercise in London?' Mark asked him. 'Squash? Jogging?'

'Squash plays havoc with one's spine, and jogging is a fad,' said Drogo. 'I don't use taxis. I walk.'

'And not only during the day,' Susie interposed, chuckling. 'A dinner date with Drogo may mean a mile's trudge to the restaurant. Girls who haven't been out with him before expect to be fetched in his car, and find that, unless it's raining *heavily*, they're expected to canter through the streets on Shanks' mare—and one has to canter to keep up. He makes no allowances for high heels.'

'I suggest they should change into walking shoes. If they choose to totter along on high heels they have only themselves to blame,' said Drogo, with a shrug.

'And they never refuse to walk with you?' Mark asked, in amazement. 'I'd expect to be told to go to hell.'

'None has refused to walk so far. But I don't delude myself that it's on account of my overwhelming personal charm,' was his cynical answer.

Annis didn't understand this remark. It seemed to her that he had a great deal of charm. But what Susie had said made it plain that Nanette could not be his wife. She must be his mistress.

'Anyway, a brisk walk there and back allows them to enjoy their dinner without worrying about putting on a pound,' he went on. 'My liking for walking seems to be regarded as an eccentricity by the media people, but I find it less freakish than jogging in Hyde Park for an hour before breakfast and then, for the rest of the day, sitting in a car or a taxi which, more often than not, is crawling along in a traffic jam.'

'Who are the media people?' Annis asked.

'Newspaper reporters, television interviewers. Talking of exercise, I'm going to swim. Who's going to join me?'

She would have joined him, but all the others said it was too soon after lunch and she did not like to be the only one to go with him.

For the Bennetts it was time to collect all the lunch things and take them back to the yacht. The two other men lit cigars while Nanette and Susie anointed themselves preparatory to stretching out on two of the sun-beds.

Diana stayed chatting to Annis who, presently, asked her, 'Is Drogo a celebrity of some sort?'

'He's a millionaire,' Diana explained. By this time her husband and brother had gone for a stroll, the girls appeared to be sleeping, and Drogo himself, after a vigorous swim, was floating with his hands clasped under his head.

'My husband is one of his senior executives,' she went on, 'and my brother is also employed by one of his companies. As you may have gathered, Mark has been in Hong Kong for several years, and is now on leave. I think—and hope—he'll be taking a bride back with him.' She lowered her voice. 'Susie is a dear girl. I know she'd make him very happy.'

'She's related to Drogo, isn't she?'

'Yes, she's a cousin on his English side. His mother was Greek, the daughter of a shipping magnate in the same league as Onassis, Livanos and Niarchos—but I suppose those names mean nothing to you. She died when Drogo was quite small, and I never met her. He's said to be like her in looks. His height and his forceful nature are from his father.'

'I thought at first Nanette was his wife.'

'Oh, no!' said Diana emphatically. 'Just a very "close friend", as they say. He isn't a marrying man. I don't think he thinks much of women.'

She was prevented from enlarging on this statement—and might not have done so—by Drogo leaving the water and rejoining them.

Annis thought it was time to take her leave, and he did not urge her to linger when she thanked him for the lunch.

As she walked up the path to the house, she was half sorry, half glad she would never see him again. Although she had enjoyed the champagne and the food, she knew it would now be harder to settle back into the unvarying routine of island life. And although Drogo Wolfe had been pleasant to her, she still felt intuitively that he was not a nice or kind man, unless it was to his advantage to assume those qualities.

She could not blame him for the fact that, by joining the lunch party, she had done something of which her father would not approve and which, if she kept it from him, would make her feel uncomfortably deceitful. That was her own fault, not Drogo's. Yet somehow it fortified her belief that he was a man of few scruples.

'The yacht is still here, I gather,' said Sylvanus, after supper that night.

Since *Sunseeker*'s anchorage was not visible from the verandah, Annis was puzzled until she saw the flash of torchlight on the path.

'Good evening, Wolfe. I trust you and your party enjoyed yourselves on the beach today?' said her father as, Annis having opened the screen door, the younger man entered.

'Very much, thank you, sir. My young cousin thought your daughter might like to look at some magazines which Susie bought to read on the flight out here, and has now finished with.'

'How very kind of your cousin. Please thank her for me,' she said, as he handed over half a dozen magazines.

'And I hope you will accept this small token of our

appreciation of being allowed to put ashore,' Drogo went on, presenting her father with what was obviously a wrapped bottle.

Annis had never heard of Glenlivet whisky, but evidently it was something special, and her father sent her to fetch two glasses in order that its donor might share his enjoyment.

'Why not three glasses?' suggested Drogo.

'A fine malt whisky is wasted on women,' was her father's dismissive reply.

As she went to fetch the two glasses, she could not help feeling a prick of resentment at his arbitrary denial that she would be able to share their appreciation.

As she returned, she was astonished to hear Drogo saying, 'Would you consider selling Morne Island, Mr Rossiter?'

'Sell the island? Certainly not! It's my home,' was her father's reply.

'Yes, and a very beautiful one. But, if I may say so, not without disadvantages for a man of your age with a young daughter to consider. Should you be taken ill, for example, how would Annis contact the outer world? Or, if she were to have an accident, how would you do so?'

'I've no doubt we should manage,' said Sylvanus. 'We're accustomed to being self-sufficient. What prompts you to ask such a question?'

'I should like the island for myself. I would pay a very good price for it.' Drogo paused, and then made an offer which made Annis gasp.

Sylvanus seemed unimpressed. 'Money means very little to us, Mr Wolfe. We have greater riches at our disposal— the wealth of the world's finest minds.'

'No doubt: but have you considered what's to become

of your daughter when you're no longer here to enjoy that wealth with her?'

'Please, Mr Wolfe ...' she protested.

'Call me Drogo, Annis.'

His smile made her flush. It was the second time that day he had told her to use his first name. Clearly he knew she had yet to tell her father about the lunch party.

'In the event of my death, my daughter will go to live with her cousin in England until such time as she can return to the island and resume her life here with a husband,' said her father. 'I've no doubt there are still some young men with the spirit to stand on their own feet, independent of all the aids of so-called civilisation.'

'I'm sure of it,' agreed Drogo. 'But have you considered that, after seeing what Europe has to offer, your daughter herself may not wish to return here?'

'Annis is as strongly attached to the island as I am,' said Sylvanus. 'She is no ordinary young woman. The trivial preoccupations of the average girl of her age would have no appeal to her.'

'I wonder?' Drogo said sceptically.

'Permit me to know my own daughter better than you, Mr Wolfe,' Sylvanus replied with a touch of asperity.

'Naturally, sir. But permit me a closer acquaintance with the realities of life. You have no boat and no radio. If you died, your daughter would be marooned with a corpse,' Drogo said brutally. 'Self-sufficient as she may be, it would be an extremely unpleasant predicament for her.'

He had voiced Annis's secret nightmare, and she was not grateful but indignant. Before she could speak, he went on, 'The price I have offered is generous. Wisely invested it would allow you to live in the seclusion you prefer but without the risks attendant here. Think it over, Mr Rossiter. I'll leave you my card in case you should wish to get in touch with me.'

'I shall not change my mind, Mr Wolfe.' Sylvanus rose from his chair. He took the card Drogo offered. 'Annis will see you out.' He disappeared into the house.

'How *could* you say that?' she accused. 'It was cruel to remind an old man that he may not live very much longer.'

'Some people would say it was cruel to keep you incarcerated here.'

'I like it here,' she retorted.

'You know nothing else,' he said dryly. 'You're a beautiful girl of nineteen, and I doubt if you've ever been kissed. Shall I remedy that for you, Annis?'

His mocking eyes seemed to mesmerise her. She wanted to back out of reach, but found herself helplessly rooted while he put his hand under her chin and tilted her face.

'Close your eyes,' he commanded softly, and she found herself doing as he bade her, conscious of nothing but his firm hold on her jaw, and the predatory gleam in his eyes before she closed hers.

She had often imagined being kissed, but never by someone like Drogo whom she scarcely knew, and mistrusted.

As his mouth closed on hers she recoiled, only to find herself clamped against his hard chest, first by one arm and then by both. To cry out, to struggle, was impossible. She could only submit, first to his superior strength, and then to her own treacherous senses which would not be controlled by her mind and responded to his skilful kiss. She felt her lips softening and parting, her tensed muscles slackening, her whole body yielding to his. Her hands, which had clenched into fists as he hauled her against him, relaxed and crept slowly upwards until they were gripping his shoulders as strongly as his hands on her.

It was he, not Annis, who brought the kiss to its abrupt conclusion. Wrenching his mouth away from hers just as she was beginning to understand how to answer the subtle persuasion of his lips moving softly on hers, he put his arms' length between them, and said, in an odd, thickened voice, 'My God! What a waste of a lovely, warm, willing girl. You were made for a young man's arms, not to nurse-maid your obstinate old father. I've a good mind to stay and show you just what you're missing. But no, better not. You'll find that out, sooner or later. Don't let him waste *all* your best years. Goodnight.'

The screen door squeaked as he opened it and let himself out.

The next time Annis emptied her father's wastepaper basket by tipping the contents into a large plastic bag to carry them to the incinerator, among the crumpled sheets of paper she saw a small slip of pasteboard which she recognised as Drogo's card.

On impulse, she retrieved it from the rest of the rubbish and later, for a reason she could not explain to herself, slipped it inside the flap inside the lid of the old brass-bound rosewood box in which she kept her few treasures.

By tacit consent neither she nor her father had made any reference to Drogo's unsettling final visit. But she knew that Sylvanus had been disturbed by the younger man's callous reference to his inevitable mortality, and her own peace of mind had been ruined by that kiss.

By day she could put it out of her mind. At night, for the first time in her life, she began to sleep badly, troubled by strange, vivid dreams interspersed with long spells of wakefulness in which she would feel his strong arms holding her captive, his experienced lips on her mouth.

About three weeks later she was down at the beach when she saw a sail on the horizon, and it was not long before she felt sure the vessel approaching the island was the yacht called *Sunseeker*. At the thought that he was returning, she began to tremble uncontrollably.

But as the yacht came to anchor in much the same place as before, Drogo was not to be seen among those on deck. Indeed, apart from the Bennetts, all those on board were strangers. Presently she saw the skipper and two male passengers lowering a box into the tender.

'We've brought you a present, young lady,' said the skipper, when he came ashore.

'A present?' she echoed, mystified.

'From your friend Mr Wolfe.' He introduced his two companions, both Americans.

Annis shook hands, impatient to learn what the present could be. She could not help feeling pleased that Drogo had not, as she had expected, forgotten her existence within hours of leaving the island.

However her pleasure was dashed when Bob Bennett explained, 'All the rest of that trip, young Miss Susie and Mr Baird's wife were worried about your being here alone with your father. They persuaded Mr Wolfe to fix you up with a radio, in case you ever need help. With the kind co-operation of our present charterers, I'm here to deliver it to you, and to show you how to operate it.'

'But surely it must cost a fortune. We can't accept it,' she began.

'Expense is no object with Mr Wolfe. He's a rich man— a very rich man. Forget the cost. Just you write him a nice letter of thanks, and be glad that from now on you won't be so dangerously isolated,' was the skipper's advice.

'Yes—yes, I will accept it, but I'm not sure about my father. You see, Mr Wolfe annoyed him by wanting to buy the island from us, and saying certain things which upset Father.'

However, Sylvanus, although at first seriously displeased by what he considered Drogo's high-handed methods in arranging delivery of the radio without any prior consultation, did not insist that it should be taken away.

'Although if Wolfe thinks this will cause me to change my mind, he is mistaken,' he told her, when they were once more on their own, but now with a link to the outer world.

As it happened, when his short, final illness occurred six months later, they were away from home and within half a mile of a hospital. But although an ambulance arrived within minutes of his collapse, and he was soon in intensive care, the outcome was the same as if it had happened on the island. Nevertheless being where they were at the time made the circumstances of his death much less harrowing for Annis.

After his funeral, she continued to stay in the guesthouse which had been their lodging on all their trips to the town. Her problem was not where to go. This had been arranged by her father in correspondence with her cousin Margaret, the daughter of his only sister.

The decision which had to be made was whether she should return to Morne Island, there to pack up the house and arrange the shipment to England of her father's library and furniture. Some enquiries with local shipping agents soon revealed that the cost would be high, and she felt her cousin might not welcome the arrival of several thousand books.

In the end she decided to leave everything as it was, and to set out for England, the scene of her future, without returning to the place which, for nineteen years and eight months, had been her haven and her prison.

On a Sunday morning a few weeks before her twenty-first birthday, Annis opened the brassbound box which, fortunately, she had had with her at the time of her father's death, and felt inside the flap for the card bearing Drogo Wolfe's name and address.

It had taken a long time to make up her mind to get in touch with him, and offer to sell the island to him. If he still wanted it. If he didn't, then someone else might. Sell it she must, if reluctantly. There was no other way to escape from the one-room flat which was her home in London, and the job which, though not uncongenial, was not what she wanted to do.

After breakfast, she went downstairs to use the coin-operated telephone installed in the hall for the use of the tenants of what, once, had been a large, gracious private house.

Her room on the first floor was part of the former drawing-room, and had the advantage of a balcony which was actually the roof of the white-columned portico which sheltered the front door. This meant that on hot summer evenings she could sit outside surrounded by the pot plants which, with the consent of the landlord, she had bought to make an oasis of greenery for herself.

The disadvantage of the room was that the partition wall which separated it from the other half of the original room was not thick enough to shut out the noise of her neighbour's television. She did not complain about it because her neighbour was a charming old lady, the widow of a general, who had come down in the world and who, being deaf, could not hear the programmes except at full volume. It had driven Annis demented until she had thought of trying out a pair of the rubber ear-plugs which some people wore when swimming. With these in place she was able to concentrate on her evening work without being disturbed by the voices and music from next door.

The voice which answered her call to the telephone number on Drogo's card was not his, but that of a man who said the number and waited for her to announce herself.

'This is Annis Rossiter. May I speak to Mr Wolfe, please?'

'Mr Wolfe no longer resides at this number, madam.'

'Oh! Do you know where he's gone?'

'I regret I am not at liberty to disclose Mr Wolfe's present residence, madam.' He sounded like a butler.

'No, I realise that, but could there be any harm in giving me his new number?'

'I believe Mr Wolfe's private number is ex-directory and known only to his intimates, madam. May I suggest you approach him through his office in the City. I can give you that number.'

Thus it was not until her lunch hour the following day that she was able to try again.

'I'll put you through to Miss Howard, who is Mr Wolfe's personal assistant. Hold the line, please,' said the switchboard operator.

A few seconds later a brisk female voice, not a young one, said 'Yes, Miss Rossiter. May I help you?'

Annis explained the situation, to which Miss Howard's response was, 'Mr Wolfe is at lunch at present, and will be in conference this afternoon. But I may be able to have a quick word with him. If you'll give me your number, I'll call you back.'

'I'm afraid I can't be reached by telephone. I finish work

at five. Will that be too late to call you back?'

'I am frequently here until eight or later,' Miss Howard replied, rather repressively. She gave the number of her extension.

The afternoon seemed much longer than usual, and Annis felt it was more than likely that, when she rang again, Miss Howard's clipped voice would inform her that Mr Wolfe thanked her for getting in touch but he was no longer interested in the purchase of Morne Island.

However, when she was put through, Miss Howard surprised her by asking, 'Do you have an engagement this evening, Miss Rossiter?'

'No ... no, I haven't.'

'In that case Mr Wolfe would like you to dine with him at his home. He is still in conference now, but hopes to be free by eight o'clock. Should he not have reached home by that time his manservant will let you in. Have you a pencil at hand, to take down the address?'

CHAPTER TWO

DROGO lived in a large block of flats with plate glass doors which slid apart to admit her when her arrival broke the beam which controlled them.

Inside she paused, glancing about her, noting the thick olive carpet, the elegant style of the chairs and sofas, the lavish arrangements of cut flowers on the two gilded console tables. If this was the vestibule, what must the apartments be like?

'Good evening, miss. Can I help you?' A smartly uniformed porter rose from a desk to assist her.

'Good evening. I'm visiting Mr Wolfe in Number Seven.'

'What name, miss?'

'Rossiter.'

'This way, Miss Rossiter.' His manner indicated that he had been warned of her coming. Clearly the residents in the block enjoyed strict security.

There were two lifts and, alongside them, glazed double doors through which Annis could glimpse a wide, close-carpeted staircase with a wrought iron balustrade topped by a shining brass handrail.

'Number Seven is the top floor, Miss Rossiter.'

The porter opened the door of one of the lifts for her.

'Thank you.' She stepped inside, and pressed the button marked 7. He had not said 'on the top floor,' which suggested that Drogo's flat occupied the whole of it.

The lift was spacious, and made to seem more so by its mirrored walls. In the few seconds' grace before she arrived, Annis looked at her reflection and wondered if she would be the first girl to cross his threshold dressed by chain stores rather than couturiers.

Luckily she had washed her hair the night before and, after speaking to Miss Howard, had had time to rush home for a quick shower in the bathroom she shared with two other tenants.

Her wardrobe was small and almost entirely composed of separates which she found the most flexible style of dressing on a tight budget. Tonight she was wearing a plain, good quality black silk tweed skirt with an emerald polyester shirt, an imitation of silk crêpe-de-chine at a third of the price of the genuine article. Her wrap for cool evenings was a black mohair shawl knitted for her, for a modest fee, by her elderly neighbour. Low-heeled black patent shoes with flat bows of black grosgrain ribbon, a small black grosgrain evening bag, and a folding black umbrella in case it should rain, completed her outfit.

She had not had her pale silky hair cut since coming to London, but had learned how to put it up in a coil at the back of her head secured by cheap plastic combs in colours to match her clothes. Tonight the combs were emerald green.

Her skin was no longer brown, but had not lost its fine, smooth texture and she wore make-up only on her eyelids and lips. Of late she had grown rather thin, which made her grey eyes, subtly shaded with a mixture of shadows, look enormous.

It seemed to Annis herself that, although she had changed little inwardly, in appearance she was scarcely recognisable as the girl who had joined Drogo Wolfe's beach party.

To a casual observer she would appear indistinguishable from the multitude of other London girls who worked in offices and stores, spent their lunch hour window-gazing and, at the end of the day, queued for buses or joined the crush in the Underground, their heads full of day-dreams about the men in their lives.

Until today Annis, too, had been in the habit of beguiling the journey home with thoughts of the man in her life. But the summons to dine with Drogo had driven him out of her mind until the last moment in the lift when she remembered that usually, at this time of night, she had thoughts for no one else.

When the lift door slid open, she stepped from it into a hall with a parquet floor overlaid with a beautiful rug. Directly in front of her stood a brilliant vermilion lacquer cabinet, its doors decorated with birds which she thought must be cranes, folded back to display the many drawers inside the cabinet, each one painted in gold with a scene from a Chinese landscape.

The gold on the drawers was repeated in the triple panels of a Greek icon, and in the grotesque features of a creature, half dragon, half dog, which guarded the door of the flat and looked to her as if it had come from a Javanese temple. Clearly, Drogo was a collector with an eclectic taste.

Remembering his kiss, at their parting twenty-one months ago, she felt suddenly stricken with nervousness, and jerked her hand back from the bell push to delay their next confrontation.

But perhaps when the lift reached this floor it triggered an early warning signal within the flat, because as she stood there, nerving herself, the door was opened by a short, dark-eyed man in black trousers and a black tie, with a coat of thin dark green material over his immaculate white shirt.

This could only be Drogo's manservant, and recalling

that his employer was half Greek on his mother's side, she took this small man to be wholly Greek.

But when he answered her shy 'Good evening', she thought she detected a slight Cockney note in his voice.

The dark brown walls of the inner hall were almost completely covered with a collection of large and small paintings at which she could only glance as the man took her wrap and umbrella and laid them aside before ushering her into a very large room overlooking an even larger roof garden.

'Mr Wolfe was delayed. He's still in the swimming pool. He thought you might also be late. Ladies aren't always as punctual as you, miss,' he said, with a smile.

Annis blinked. 'There's a swimming pool up here?'

'This way, miss.'

He led Annis round the corner to a part of the L-shaped room where, through floor-to-ceiling windows, she could see a large pool in which someone was swimming a fast crawl with a beautiful stylishness of stroke which she remembered from seeing Drogo swim once before.

'Mr Wolfe likes to swim fifty lengths night and morning. He should be nearly finished by now.'

Even as he spoke Drogo reached the far end of the pool and hauled himself out. His back was as brown as before, from which she concluded that, unlike herself, he had been in the sun very often since their last meeting.

Still turned away from his onlookers, he picked up and shrugged himself into a long white towelling robe with a hood which, when it was in place, he rubbed briskly over his hair. Then he stepped into towelling mules, looking, Annis thought, like a tall desert monk in the habit-like robe with its belt of thick white cotton rope.

At this point the small man moved towards the windows

which, like the entrance doors on the ground floor, slid aside to let him advance on to the flagged walk round the pool.

She heard him say, 'Miss Rossiter is here, sir.'

At this Drogo turned, looking past his butler to where she remained in the room with a thumping heart and dry mouth.

He came towards her, pushing the hood off his head, a bright drop of water leaving the end of one eyebrow and trailing down the prominent slant of his cheekbone to where the lean, taut brown cheek was seamed by the crease which appeared whenever, as now, he was smiling.

'Annis!' He came as far as the threshold of the windows where he halted and held out his hand.

As she moved forward to take it, he looked her over, taking in the sophisticated hair and make-up, the undating simplicity of her clothes, the slenderness of her ankles in sheer black tights.

When she put her hand into his, he said softly, 'Annis grown up,' and, instead of shaking her hand, he raised it and kissed her knuckles, holding them to his lips a good deal longer than was necessary, his hazel eyes fixed on hers and, in them, the very same gleam she remembered from last time.

Then he let her hand fall and straightened, saying, 'I expect Theron has told you I was held up. I shan't keep you more than five minutes. While I'm dressing, what will you drink?'

'Oh ... I'll wait for you,' she replied, her ability to think of a drink blanked out by the powerful force of his personality.

'In that case we'll both have a Hintlesham White Lady, Theron.'

Left on her own, Annis wandered around the vast room

which was full of fascinating objects and interesting paintings superimposed on a background of serene neutrality and infinite luxury.

Knowing the price of her plain silk tweed skirt, on which she had splurged because it was an important basic which she expected to wear for season after season, her mind boggled at the cost of the hundreds of metres of much heavier quality cream silk tweed, lined and interlined with thick, soft bump, and completely hand-sewn, which would later be drawn across the windows. The carpet, which exactly matched the curtains, was as thick and springy as moss overlaid, in front of the fire, with an oriental rug.

But the thing which struck her most forcibly was the soothing silence. When a fine old longcase clock chimed the quarter hour, the first note actually startled her.

She was startled again, a few moments later, when Drogo asked, 'Do you like it?', and she turned to find him in the room with her, his footsteps made soundless by the dense pile of the carpet and its thick underlay.

She had, when he spoke, been gazing at a small porcelain statuette of a girl in a Grecian tunic with a garland of flowers on her hair. The dress was white and slightly glazed, but the rest of the figure was pale matt celadon green. On the circular base on which the figure was standing was written *Canova*.

'It's a rather rare Minton copy of Canova's *Dancing Girl*,' said Drogo, coming to look at it with her. 'Canova, as you may know, was the Italian sculptor who took plaster casts of the beautiful breasts of Napoleon's favourite sister so that she wouldn't have to pose while he sculpted them for his famous statue of her as the Venus Victrix.'

'No, I didn't know that. H-how interesting,' Annis murmured.

It was stupidly gauche to feel flurried by his mention of

breasts in such an impersonal context, yet she had the unnerving conviction that, having mentioned them impersonally, now he was looking at hers, half outlined by the emerald green shirt.

She was glad when Theron appeared.

'What is in this?' she asked, as she took a glass from the tray which the manservant offered her.

'It's Robert Carrier's variation on the White Lady cocktail invented at Harry's New York bar which opened in Paris way back in 1911. Have you been to Carrier's restaurant in Camden Passage?'

She shook her head.

'I must take you. I think you'd like it. Carrier is a well-known gourmet and cookery writer. I haven't met him, but I believe he's an American by birth and a European by inclination. He also has a fine country house, Hintlesham Hall in Suffolk, which is partly his home and partly a restaurant. The original White Lady cocktail was two measures of gin to one of lemon juice and one of Cointreau. Carrier's version is gin and lemon juice in equal quantities, a dash of Cointreau and a pinch of sugar, all vigorously shaken with the white of an egg and ice. I usually have one before dinner. See what you think of it.'

Annis sipped. Her knowledge of alcohol was limited to an occasional glass of sherry when she invited her neighbour to share her supper, or a carafe of cheap plonk in a pizza bar or a steak house after going a theatre or concert with one of the several impecunious young men who had dated her before she had begun, pleasantly but firmly, to refuse all further dates.

She had a feeling that any mixture which included gin and a liqueur must be heady stuff which deserved to be drunk with some caution.

'It's very good,' she said politely.

'Come and sit down.'

Drogo led the way to the group of three creamy suede sofas which formed a square with the chimney wall. This looked as if it had come from a Georgian house, now demolished. It was made of pale golden pine, with garlands and borders of carved wood forming panels on either side of the projecting chimney-breast, on which a similar panel was filled with a large marine painting of two clipper ships racing each other.

Drogo waited for her to sit down before he seated himself. He was dressed in pale grey pants and a V-necked blouson top of velvety cotton velours of a slightly darker shade of grey, with a colourful silk scarf filling the neck. His footwear was equally colourful, for he was shod in a pair of scarlet and black *petit point* slippers, with grey silk socks. Annis wondered who had embroidered the slippers for him. The overall effect was comfortable, casual and yet stylish. She had the impression that he paid some attention to his choice of clothes in the first place, but not much thereafter. He had dressed as quickly as he had promised. No dandy would have reappeared in so short a time.

'Bring me up to date with your life,' he said. 'You've been in London some time, I should think, looking at you. No "noble savage" achieved such a high degree of polish in a matter of weeks.'

'Yes, I've been here over a year. My father died about six months after you made us that wonderfully generous present of the radio. I hope you received our letter of thanks.'

'I received *your* letter of thanks,' he said dryly. 'I shouldn't have expected your father to be too pleased by what he no doubt regarded as an act of presumptuous arrogance.'

The colour which stained her pale cheeks confirmed

his shrewd guess at Sylvanus Rossiter's reaction. He grinned, and said, 'However, we won't go into that.'

'No, but I did think afterwards, when I made the decision to leave all our things on the island, that I should have written to you and arranged the return of the radio. The reason I didn't was that I thought, if I told you my father had died, you might think I was angling for more help—which wouldn't have been the case at all.'

'I'm sure it wouldn't,' he acknowledged. 'Had you been among the world's spongers, you'd have been in touch with me long since. What are the circumstances which have made you decide now that you want to dispose of the island? Do you find you prefer life in England? Or is your preference for one particular Englishman?'

She hesitated. 'In a way—yes.'

His question had made her think that it might be strategically sound to let him suppose she had some emotional involvement, as indeed she had—but not of the kind he would envisage.

'I seem to recall your father telling me that after his death you would be given a home by some relation over here.'

'Yes, by Cousin Margaret. I did stay with her for some weeks.'

'It didn't work out?'

Annis shook her head. She had seated herself on the sofa facing the small log fire which added its leaping flamelight to the roseate glow of various table lamps. She was sitting with both feet on the floor. But Drogo, although not unnervingly close to her, had only one foot on the carpet. The other was resting on the seat cushion, tucked under the long, strong thigh of his other leg as he sat turned towards her, his glass held in his right hand while his left hand lay on the backrest, not far from her shoulder.

Glancing at him only now and then, but conscious of being all the time under his searching scrutiny, had made her forget her intention to sip her drink slowly. No doubt it was the strong cocktail which undermined her resolve to tell him as little as possible about herself.

When he asked her, 'What was she like?', she found herself saying, 'She's the daughter of Father's elder sister, so she's now about fifty. She's built like a sergeant-major, with a very loud voice, and she sits on a lot of committees and breeds revolting little dogs which never stop yapping. I——'

She stopped short, rather regretting this unflattering description of her only living relation.

Drogo seemed amused. He said, 'And I imagine the reason your cousin offered you a home was not from any warmhearted desire to give shelter to a young kinswoman with nowhere else to turn, but from a pressing need for a useful and unpaid factotum?'

'Yes, exactly that! How did you guess?'

He shrugged. 'Experience of life.'

'Was this charmer an unmarried woman, or did she have a husband?' he asked.

'Oh, yes, and he was the last straw.'

'He made advances to you?'

'Yes.'

'With a wife like that one can hardly blame him.'

'She can't have been like that always, or he wouldn't have married her. Anyway, I couldn't stay with them, and I didn't much like their part of the country, so I came to London and lived in a hostel until I found myself a job and a place to live. And of course as soon as I moved I began to enjoy life tremendously because of all the marvellous things to see here.'

Drogo was about to put a question to her when Theron

appeared round the corner from the part of the room where, earlier, Annis had noticed two places laid at a large dining table.

'Dinner is served, sir.'

Drogo took her empty glass from her and put it on the low glass table between the sofa. 'Have you had any more caviar since I gave you your first taste of it?' he enquired.

'No, it's way outside my budget. I've been told that it can cost as much as one hundred and twenty-eight pounds a pound! Can that be true?'

'Probably. Theron's wife is such a first-rate cook that I rarely go to restaurants. But I was a guest in a fish place in Knightsbridge Green recently where I noticed they were charging thirty pounds for a hundred grams of Beluga caviar, although on the same menu they had thirty grams of pressed caviar, served with blinis and sour cream, for under five pounds. My own caviar is supplied direct from its source without any middlemen making extortionate profits. However much money one has, there's no point in lining other men's pockets beyond what is reasonable,' he added, as he held her chair for her.

The long table could have seated a dozen people. The two places laid on it now were on either side of the centre, with vases of early daffodils and imported mimosa set apart so that they did not impede his view of her, or hers of him.

'We're not having caviar tonight but, in your honour, Rosie has prepared a seafood supper for us, starting with this bisque de homard,' he went on, as Theron served a lobster soup with an aroma which reminded Annis that her usual supper-time was seven, and it was now half past eight.

'What are the blinis you mentioned a moment ago?' she asked, unfolding a napkin of pale yellow lined to match the table-mats.

In a single glance she noticed that the soup plate, the plate beneath it, and the side plate were white with an intricate border of gold. The cutlery was antique silver. The water and wine glasses shining in the soft candlelight were not of cut crystal but plain, except for a band of delicate engraving near their rims.

'They're Russian pancakes which have yeast in them,' Drogo told her.

When the butler had left them, she said, 'Rosie doesn't sound like a Greek name. Is Theron's wife English?'

'As he is, except by descent. He was born in London of Greek parents. Rosie is a Battersea girl, but an international cook. I'm lucky to have them looking after me. Where do you live, and with whom?'

'In Pimlico, by myself. Being accustomed to solitude, I didn't think I should like sharing a flat with other girls, although I know that, by doing that, one can usually get better accommodation for less rent.'

'Some girls—particularly the good-looking ones—solve the accommodation problem by sharing a place with only one other person, not of their own sex,' he said.

Annis looked up from the soup, her grey eyes meeting his with a slightly frosty expression. 'Some may, I don't.'

'So you live in Pimlico, and work—where?'

When she told him the name of the store where she worked in the cosmetics department, he raised his eyebrows.

'Is that the best job you could find?'

'I didn't want to work in an office, and a lot of the interesting jobs are closed to me because I haven't any certificates to prove that I've been well educated. I wanted to live by myself, but to work where I'd mix with plenty of people. The woman at the employment agency suggested my present job to me. She said the cosmetics firms like girls with unblemished skins on their counters as an advertisement for their products.'

'Yes, you have an excellent skin—probably because until recently you never used any cosmetics.'

'It's not using them which causes trouble. It's the failure to clean them off properly.' Her face lit with sudden amusement. 'Or maybe that's just a piece of customer brainwash which has washed off on me. Anyway, since I got used to the high level of heating in the store—somehow artificial heat is quite different from natural heat—I've found the job quite enjoyable. I'm selling an expensive brand, and a lot of the rich women who buy it pour out other troubles besides their make-up problems. It's extraordinary how many women with furs and jewels, and chauffeur-driven cars waiting outside for them, are so unhappy and lonely that they'll confide in a salesgirl. I don't really envy the——' She broke off in sudden confusion.

'You don't envy the rich,' he finished for her. 'No, why should you? You're young and beautiful. You've no need to envy anyone. But those women you speak of aren't unhappy because of their riches, but in spite of them. You would encounter just as many dissatisfied women in any of London's street markets. It's in people's natures either to be happy or unhappy, and a happy person will be even happier with money because, although *some* of the best things in life are free, others are extremely expensive.'

Theron came to remove the soup plates and serve the next course which was one of his wife's specialities, baked herrings *à la Calaisienne*, which were stuffed with their own roes mixed with shallots and parsley. They were served with *maître d'hotel* butter, and a pale golden, very dry wine which, said Drogo, was a Tocai from vineyards an hour north of Venice.

'Is that how you met your boy-friend?—When he came to buy scent for someone else, and was charmed by the salesgirl?' he asked her, as they ate the fish.

'No ... I came across him in a junk shop near where I live.'

'It must be serious if you're thinking of renouncing Morne Island for him. Was that his idea?'

'My cousin and her husband are the only people who know I own an island. They tried to persuade me to sell it, but at that time I didn't want to. Now I realise it just isn't practicable to keep it. I don't like going against Father's wishes. But it's common sense.'

His hazel eyes studied her thoughtfully for some moments before he asked, 'Why isn't it practicable to keep the island?'

'How can I earn my living there? My father had a small State pension which died with him. Not long ago I had a letter from my mother's publishers to say that her history book which has been in print for years has finally been superseded, so there won't be any more royalties from it, or none worth mentioning. I have to stay here and work; and that's what I want to do anyway, only with a cottage in the country where I can go for weekends. The sale of the island would pay for that and various other things. I would have gone direct to a firm which deals with overseas property, but as you had once been interested, and after your great kindness to us, I felt it was only right to give you the first option on it.'

'Thank you. I appreciate your consideration.' He added some wine to her glass, and refilled his own.

'But perhaps after leaving our island, you found another

you liked which *was* for sale?' she suggested.

'No, I let the whole idea slide. Now ... well, I'm not sure. I'll have to think the thing over. How long can you give me to reconsider?'

'As long as you wish.'

'A fortnight?'

'By all means.'

'Then we'll dine again, two weeks from now, and I'll give you a firm decision on it.'

'Thank you, that would be fine,' she smiled. 'I won't suggest that we dine *chez moi* on that occasion because, although I'm teaching myself to be a better cook, it will be a long time before I'm in the same league as Rosie—if ever.'

'And no doubt your boy-friend wouldn't like it if he called and found you entertaining another man. Where does he think you are this evening?'

'I don't devote every evening to him.'

'Wise girl: never let a man know you're hooked until you're sure he's hooked.'

'Isn't that rather a cold-blooded concept?' she objected. 'And an old-fashioned one as well. We don't have to "hook" men any more. We're no longer dependent on your sex for a home and status. We need men on an equal basis, for love, companionship and children.'

Drogo's mouth took a mocking slant. 'I can see it's not only the cosmetic manufacturers' propaganda which has washed off on you. That's a Women's Lib spiel,' was his bantering comment.

Annis opened her mouth to deliver a vigorous riposte, but was checked by Theron's return.

The pudding was as delicious as the preceding courses: a brandy gâteau of which Theron cut a slice which caused his employer to remonstrate, 'Miss Rossiter isn't slimming. If anything, she needs building up.'

Whereupon she was cut a much larger slice.

Drogo's reference to her thinner figure reminded her how, on the island, she had feared that she might be too curvy.

'How is Susie? Is she married to David?' she asked, as her fork probed the crust of nibbed almonds to gather up the fresh redcurrants between the sponge base and the topping of cream whipped with brandy.

'Yes, and living in Hong Kong.'

'And Mr and Mrs Baird, and Nanette?'

'The Bairds are well. Nanette ...' He shrugged. 'I don't know. It's a long time since I last saw her.'

Without stopping to think, Annis said, 'I suppose she forgot your maxim, and allowed herself to be hooked before you were hooked by her.'

'There was never the smallest chance that I should be,' he answered.

'Perhaps she didn't know that.'

'Oh, yes, she knew it. I play fair with women. I make my intentions clear from the outset—and they're always strictly dishonourable.'

Was there a note of warning underlying this cynical statement? If so, it was unnecessary. Annis had never trusted this man, and she didn't now, convinced that his gift of the radio had been prompted by Diana Baird and Susie, not by his own concern for her.

To conclude their meal, Theron brought in a whole Camembert with some other cheeses in case she should not like the rich Norman one which bore on its crust the marks of the straw on which it had matured.

But the food halls of the store where she worked were

famous for the provision of all manner of gourmets' delights. Although Annis could not afford to buy many things there, now and then she would treat herself to a small amount of a fine cheese, and one of the men at the cheese counter had imparted some of his knowledge to her. Thus she knew that pre-packed halves seldom ripened well, and that a cheese which had sunk or one with a hard edge was either over-ripe or over-refrigerated.

Knowing that any cheese presented at Drogo's table would be of the very best quality, she said, 'Oh, Camembert, please,' when Theron looked enquiringly at her.

The piece which he placed on a plate for her was oozing under the crust but still slightly crumbly at its heart. After looking appreciatively at it, she glanced up to find Drogo watching her with a faint smile. His expression made her realise that an instant before, involuntarily, she had licked her lips. Considering how well she had dined already, no wonder he was amused at her greed for the cheese.

'We'll have coffee by the fire, Theron,' he said.

For the next few minutes there was silence as they both concentrated on what she had once heard another customer at the cheese counter call 'the smell of heaven'.

Then, snapping a second crisp biscuit between his long, well-shaped fingers, he remarked, 'Now that we've concluded our business discussion for the time being, we can devote ourselves to pleasure.'

What did *that* mean? she wondered apprehensively.

Aloud, she said, 'Apropos what you were saying about some of the best things in life being expensive, I've realised since coming to England what a very great luxury silence is. Living in London, it's almost impossible to escape some background noise. Even in the centre of Hyde Park, there's always the distant drone of traffic. But you seem to have achieved silence up here—apart from the crackling of the fire and the ticking of the clock which are soothing sounds.'

'Yes, I can't stand perpetual noise. It's said that many of your generation are going to be prematurely deaf. Their ears are being damaged in discotheques where the decibel level is so high that, were it their place of work, they would have to wear ear-muffs.'

'I've only been once to a disco,' said Annis, 'and I didn't like it. How irresponsible of the managements of those places to allow it to go on at that level.'

'Where profits are involved, scruples go down the drain,' he said dryly. 'It takes different forms nowadays, but I sometimes think the great mass of the population are as much exploited as they ever were, but it's done much more subtly nowadays.'

Annis said, 'Talking of exploitation, one of the staff in our carpet department told me that although, officially, it's illegal for children to be apprenticed in carpet factories before they're twelve, in fact the Anti-Slavery Society has discovered that in Morocco, there are still little girls of eight or nine who work for seventy-two hours a week for a dollar a day. I can see all your rugs are old ones, so you're not a party to it. But people who buy modern rugs which were made in Morocco may, unwittingly, be helping to keep those children in slavery.'

'Yes, the world is full of black deeds, but I think we need not depress ourselves with them this evening,' he said, with a tinge of impatience. 'Let's go and relax by the fire, shall we? I'll play you some mood music.'

This sounded even more ominous. She said, hoping her nervousness was not audible in her voice, 'Before that, would you mind if I went to the kitchen for a minute, to tell Rosie how very much I've enjoyed her delicious cooking?'

'No need to go to the kitchen. I'll send for her.'

'What's her name? Her surname?'

'Patronicolous.'

When Theron came in with the coffee tray, Drogo asked him to summon his wife. Rosie Patronicolous was of even shorter stature than her husband; a little, round, rosy-faced woman in a neat dark green short-sleeved overall of the same material as his jacket.

'Miss Rossiter wishes to compliment you, Rosie,' explained Drogo.

Not caring if it was 'done' or not, Annis stood up and held out her hand, saying warmly, 'How do you do, Mrs Patronicolous. I couldn't leave without telling you how much I've enjoyed every mouthful of that wonderful meal—especially the herrings.'

'It's very kind of you to say so, miss. It's quite a simple dish, really. When I was a kiddy, herrings was a poor people's fish, but not these days, if they're nicely presented.'

Annis opened her mouth to reply, but was forestalled by Drogo who said, 'If you wish to take Rosie to see her sister, Theron, we shan't need you again.'

'I should like to pop across for a couple of hours, if you're sure it's convenient, Mr Wolfe,' said Rosie.

'Perfectly. Give Rita my good wishes.'

'Thank you, sir. Goodnight, miss.' Rosie withdrew, and Theron disappeared round the corner to clear the dining table.

Conscious that this was a task which would not take him more than a few minutes, after which they would be alone in the room and, not long afterwards, alone in the apartment, Annis perched on the extreme edge of the sofa. As she drank the coffee which Theron had poured for her, she watched, with inward disquiet, Drogo choosing a record from a large library of them concealed in the section of wall which also housed an elaborate music centre.

Since having to deal with her cousin's husband's unwelcome fondlings, she had taken care to avoid situations which gave men a chance to pounce on her.

She had no experience of handling the type of determinedly amorous approach which she thought Drogo had in mind, and the situation was made more than ordinarily fraught by the fact that she did not want to offend a man who would probably pay her a better price for the island than anyone else.

To her surprise, and temporary relief, the record he had chosen was not the soft, sexy music she had expected. When she asked what it was, he said, 'Stravinsky's *Rite of Spring.*'

While she was listening to it, feeling that she could relax at least until it ended, Drogo opened another cupboard and presently brought her a glass with a colourless liqueur in it. Feeling that any time now she was going to need all her wits, Annis took only a token sip of it.

For a while he strolled round the room, drinking what appeared to be cognac, and gazing with a connoisseur's pleasure upon the many handsome objects which, because the room was so spacious, were displayed to their best advantage without any feeling of overcrowding. But by the time the music ended he had come back to sit near Annis.

'Where is it that Rosie is popping across to?' she enquired, in a bright, conversational tone.

'To the other side of the river where the rest of her family still lives. Her much younger sister, Rita, has just given birth to twins, and Rosie likes to go over and lend a hand as often as possible.'

'Twins babies must be quite a handful. Are they boys or girls, or one of each?' she asked, in a strained play for time.

It was still only half past nine. She could not make her escape yet.

'I believe they're identical girls. I see you glancing at the clock. Tomorrow being a weekday, I imagine you don't want to be too late getting home?'

Was he making fun of her? Could he tell she was nervous of him?

'No. I'm a lark, not an owl. I still tend to rise at first light, and to go to bed fairly early.'

She thought of a way to elude him for five or six minutes.

'May I use your bathroom?' she asked.

'Of course.' He showed her where it was.

Safely locked in the green marble bathroom, Annis took as long as she dared to wash her hands and repair her lipstick. But she couldn't stay there indefinitely.

When at length she emerged from sanctuary, Drogo was lounging by the fire, his long legs crossed, his muscular shoulders relaxed against the plump, feather-filled cushions.

When he saw her returning, he rose. 'I have the distinct impression that you're rather frightened of me, Annis.'

'F-frightened of you?' she echoed.

'That I may be going to make love to you.'

'Well ... I hope not,' she answered, her voice not quite steady.

'Why? Because the boy-friend wouldn't like it? But you would, I think, if you're honest.'

She didn't know how he contrived it, but as she moved

to sit down, with one swift stride he had intercepted and captured her.

And he was right: she did like it. The strong arms enfolding her body, the warm lips closing on hers were the right and natural conclusion to the evening's other sensual pleasures: good food, wine, music, and all the visual delights of the now firelit room.

His previous kiss, on the island, had been almost a rape—unexpected, violent, enforcing rather than persuading. This time it was different. His kiss was gentle and coaxing. And she was older, ready and ripe for this experience.

Drogo drew her down on to the sofa, cradling her across his legs while his kisses explored her throat, and returned to her lips a little less gently than before.

In a part of her mind she was conscious of the skill with which, slowly, slowly, he infiltrated her resistance. Each kiss, like an incoming tide, was a slight advance on its precursor, each touch a little more intimate.

His hand stroked her neck, her shoulder, and then, very lightly, her breast, protected by two layers of fabric. She was only dimly aware of his practised fingers unfastening the front of her shirt because, at the same time, his mouth had become more demanding.

Her bra was a front-fastening wisp of translucent white shimmer-nylon. She would have expected a man to be defeated by the plastic clip between the under-wired cups. It had to be bent at an angle before it could be unfastened. Perhaps Drogo had encountered it before, for with one deft flick he had it open, and her quivering breasts bare to his touch.

'No ... no ... you mustn't,' she begged, as his hands explored the soft flesh which he had exposed.

His lips became suddenly fierce, stifling her protests, making her shudder and squirm to escape his strong arm.

'Why not? It's what we both want. To hell with the boy-friend,' he murmured huskily.

With her last ounce of will-power Annis wrenched herself free and sprang up, clutching her shirt over her nakedness. She would not have believed it was possible to want a man's hands to caress her as keenly as she wanted his to continue their skilled exploration. He was almost a stranger: her wantonness shocked and appalled her.

'If I'd known this was why you'd asked me here, I shouldn't have come,' she flared angrily, over her shoulder. She had her back to him now, and was fumbling to right her disordered clothing.

'It wasn't the reason I asked you here. But now that I've seen you again, I want you as much as before, when you were a virgin.'

'I still am,' she panted, trembling.

'You can't be serious? At your age? With your looks?'

'Is it so unusual?'

'I should say it's extremely unusual. I don't believe it.'

'You'll have to take my word for it, I'm a virgin, and I mean to remain one until ... until I'm in love,' she retorted, her soft voice unsteady, her trembling hands making it impossible for her to re-fasten the clip.

Drogo had remained on the sofa, and she had not realised he could see what she was doing in a mirror. Suddenly she found him close behind her, saying, 'You'd better let me deal with that for you.'

'No! Don't touch me!'

She would have fled from him again, but he caught her and held her still with her arms to her sides and her shirt still open so that he could see in the mirror the agitated rise and fall of her breasts.

'I shouldn't have thought you needed a bra. You have excellent natural uplift—as I noticed the first time I saw you.'

Scarlet-cheeked, she made futile attempts to free herself, kicking backwards at his shins but failing to make contact. 'You beast—let me go!' she panted.

'You should have protested sooner. One thing leads to another, my girl. Even a virgin should know that. Or is your boy-friend so tame that he lets you arouse him with kisses, but never goes further? If so, it's high time you learnt that not all men are equally tractable.' Holding her captive with one arm, he began to caress her again. 'Don't worry, I'm not going to test your claim to virginity,' he mocked. 'But you should have made it clear from the outset.'

'How? I didn't invite you to kiss me. You gave me no choice,' she stormed at him, her continued struggles to break free from this new hold as useless as those before.

'And you quickly responded, my dear—as you're doing now, in spite of your protests.'

He looked down over her shoulder at the twin annulets of darker skin, their damask centres no longer soft to his touch but projecting like rosy buds from the ivory globes of her now untanned breasts.

'If you are still a virgin, it must be a hell of a strain to preserve that unfashionable status when you react as rapidly as this to a little gentle love-play,' he taunted her.

'You swine! How dare you!' she raged.

'I'm enjoying it. So are you really.'

'I'm not. I hate it ... I hate it!' She closed her eyes to shut out the sight of his brown hand cupping her naked breast while his thumb teased its peak.

But closing her eyes, she discovered, only served to make her more aware of the strong male body behind her, the lips which were nibbling her ear, and the warm, expert hand which had forced a response from her flesh which her mind repudiated.

When his lips moved round to her nape a low groan broke from her. She felt his teeth softly biting the back of her neck, and a long shudder racked her, not of the revulsion she wanted to feel, but of a voluptuous pleasure such as she had never experienced before. Her skin crawled, but not with loathing. Strange spasms began to contract her stomach and thighs. Her whole body seemed to pulsate in time with her wildly beating heart. She no longer squirmed and struggled, but stood passively inside the arm which held her, her head bending forward under the searching pressure of his mouth on her neck, her resistance finally evaporated less by his superior physical strength than by his understanding of her body, and how he could make it betray her.

All at once it was over. 'Too much more of this and you won't be a virgin tomorrow,' Drogo murmured sardonically, as he found the two sides of her bra and brought them together, slotting the bar of the clip into the tube which secured it.

After one last caress with both hands he moved away, saying calmly, 'I'd better take you home. Did you have a coat?'

'A sh-shawl,' she answered unsteadily.

'I'll fetch it.'

By the time he came back she had buttoned her shirt and recovered her bag from the floor where she had let it fall when he had taken her in his arms.

Striving for a measure of self-possession but unable to meet his eyes, she said stiffly, 'It isn't necessary to see me home. The porter will get me a taxi.'

'And think me an unchivalrous fellow to send off a young

woman guest alone in a cab,' was Drogo's reply, as he put the shawl round her shoulders.

'Well, you aren't chivalrous, are you?' she retorted, on a bitter note.

'I try to appear so in public. It's only in private that I show my true colours,' he answered mockingly. 'Don't give me that Sabine glare. I haven't done anything very terrible to you. Had you grown up with other young people, you'd have had as much kissing and petting by the time you were sixteen or seventeen.'

'But not imposed on me by force,' was her angry riposte.

'Your sex likes a certain amount of force. If a man asks a girl if he may kiss her, she feels obliged to say no. The Women's Libbers wouldn't agree but, basically, you're all cave-women who would rather be dragged by the hair than treated with too much respect,' he informed her casually.

Speechless with indignation, she stalked past him towards the hall. But the outer door had a latch which she had to wait for him to open for her, and she could not prevent him from following her into the lift. It was not until the door opened and outside it she saw, not the lobby, but an underground garage, that she realised he had not pressed the button marked G.

'Don't argue. I'm driving you home—with both hands on the wheel,' he added, slanting a quizzical glance at her set face and hostile eyes.

He led her across to a sleek white Ferrari Boxer parked between a Bentley and a Mercedes which might also be his for all she knew. Reluctantly Annis got in. Inside, it smelt of the real leather of the upholstery. She had never been a passenger in a de luxe car before, but was too upset and enraged to admire the expensive details which distinguished it from an ordinary car.

It was still not quite ten o'clock, and the traffic in the

streets was lighter than it would be later, when the theatres and cinemas had closed.

The drive did not take very long, but it seemed interminable to her. Although the heater was on, and she had the light but snug shawl clutched across her still tingling breasts, she could not stop shivering as if she were starting a chill. She supposed it must be a nervous reaction to the shock of his unscrupulous behaviour.

Near where she lived she had to give him some directions.

'This corner will do,' she said brusquely, at the end of her street.

'I was brought up always to see girls safely to their front door,' was Drogo's reply to this. 'But in the circumstances, I shan't expect you to invite me in for a nightcap,' he added, taking his eyes off the road for a moment.

She kept hers fixed straight ahead, but on the periphery of her vision she saw the flash of his teeth as a grin accompanied his sally.

'I live at Number Eleven,' she told him frigidly.

Both sides of the street were lined with the cars of residents. There was no space for him to park, and she hoped to jump out the moment he stopped and never to see him again. But once again her intention was frustrated by difficulty in opening the door so that, by the time she had managed it, he had walked round the bonnet to hold it for her. However, he had left the engine running so she had no fear he might try to enter the house with her.

'You'll hardly expect me to thank you for a pleasant evening,' she said icily, as they mounted the steps to the portico.

She regretted her lack of foresight in not getting out her key before they arrived.

'It was not all unpleasant, was it?' he asked her dryly.

Annis thrust her key into the lock, and turned to face him, her eyes bright with angry contempt.

'The last part was hateful,' she told him. 'And you can forget the island. I'd rather die than sell it to you!'

'I think you should sleep on that decision. Goodnight, Annis. Sweet dreams.' With that curiously foreign bow, and a smile which showed he was unconvinced by her wrath, Drogo turned and went back to the car.

When, the next day, she woke to rain, she realised her umbrella was in his apartment. He had not known she had it with her, and she had been too distressed and humiliated to remember it.

She was able to borrow a brolly from her elderly neighbour, who remarked, 'You look very tired, Annis.'

It was not to be wondered at, she thought, on her way to work. She had had less than three hours' sleep, kept awake by the shaming memory of how easily Drogo had overcome her resistance. If he had tried to seduce her, would he have succeeded? That was something she would never know. Although he had spoken as if they would meet again, she was determined to avoid a second encounter. She could not trust herself with him.

At lunch time she went to the office of an estate agency with international connections, and arranged for them to sell Morne Island. The price they thought it might fetch was more than Drogo had offered, but much as she wanted to think the worst of him, her intelligence told her that this was not so much because he had tried to do down her father as because of the soaring rise in world inflation since that time.

It was still raining when the store closed. Annis planned

to have a light supper and go to bed early, to catch up on
the sleep lost last night. After supper she had a bath, and
presently wished she had not, for as she lay in the water,
the sight of her half-submerged body was an unwelcome
reminder of Drogo's bronzed hand making love to her.
Except that it hadn't been love but lust which had prompted his caresses. It was obvious that he regarded all women
as playthings. Diana Baird had said as much that day
they had lunched on the island.

It had been naïve, she saw now, not to guess that an
invitation to his flat would end precisely as it had ended.
After the way he had kissed her in the West Indies, she had
only herself to blame for what had occurred at his apartment.

Recalling what he had said about her virginity being remarkable in view of her sensuous nature, she wondered
why no other man's kiss had ever stirred her as his had.
Her cousin's husband had been old and unattractive, but
most of the men who had taken her about in London had
been good-looking young men whose goodnight kisses she
had enjoyed without being in any danger of losing her
head.

All the tenants at Number Eleven had a bell with their
name-card outside the front door. Above these there was
a device which enabled them to ask callers to identify
themselves before the door was unlocked for them.

Annis was ready for bed, and was drinking a cup of hot
chocolate to help her to sleep, when she was startled by
someone ringing her bell. Thinking it must be a mistake,
for she knew of no one who would call on her on such a
night, she asked who it was.

'Drogo,' his deep voice answered.

'What do you want?' she asked shortly.

'I've brought back your umbrella, and I'd like to talk for five minutes.'

'You can't,' she said baldly. 'Please leave the umbrella by the door.'

For some moments afterwards she was afraid he would continue to ring the bell until she was forced to go down. But he didn't, yet nor did she hear the sound of his car driving away. Perhaps, as was often the case, the street was already fully parked, and Drogo had had to leave his car some distance away.

On impulse she went to the window and drew back the curtain to see if she could glimpse him retreating along the wet street.

The rain was bucketing down even more heavily than when she had left work. The light of the street lamp on the opposite pavement showed how heavily it was falling. It also revealed the tall figure of a man in a black oilskin raincoat and rubber boots. Although his body and his feet were protected from the downpour, his dark head was bare.

As she stared at him, with a strange perturbation, he took one hand out of the pocket of the seamanlike waterproof coat and waved to her. Then he turned and began to move away, not hurrying as most people would in a deluge, but striding at an ordinary pace, apparently heedless of the heavy rain beating down on his uncovered head.

As she let the curtain fall into place, Annis recognised that her reaction to seeing him standing there had been a quite unnecessary sense of concern. If Drogo chose to walk about London in heavy rain, there was no reason why she should feel unkind and ungracious for refusing to admit him to what, now the cover was removed from the studio couch, was in effect her bedroom.

Putting a dressing-gown over her sleeping suit of apricot brushed cotton jersey, she went downstairs to retrieve her umbrella from the porch.

Although Drogo had shaken most of the water from it, he had used it on his way to her, probably not to cover himself so much as to shield the beautiful white azalea which she found on the doorstep beside it. The plant had a transparent wrapping inside which there was a small envelope of the kind supplied by florists to contain a card from the donor of a floral present.

In her room, Annis unwrapped the plant which was in full and perfect flower, and opened the envelope on which was written *A. R. First Floor.* From this she concluded that, after returning to his car the night before, he must have waited to see her light go on. On the card inside the envelope, there was nothing except his initials scrawled with a thick-tipped black fibre pen, the bold letters very much in style with the man who had written them.

The next day she came home to find that her elderly neighbour had taken delivery for her of a charming little obelisk-shaped bay tree such as Annis had often admired outside houses in fashionable mews, and knew to be far beyond her pocket.

She was unwilling to accept such an expensive gift from him; although, from his point of view, she knew the cost of the trees was probably a trifling addition to his account with Moyses Stevens, the West End florists through whose eye-catching windows, down which a transparent curtain of water streamed, she had often gazed at long-stemmed pink roses and wonderful cyclamens and fuchsias.

Eventually the difficulty of taking it on a bus, the unwelcome expense of the taxi fare from her neighbourhood to his, and the arm-racking labour of carrying it to his apartment to leave it with the porter, made her resign herself to keeping it.

The following day was her day off, and she was at home to receive a lavish bouquet of all-white flowers. This time the envelope with them was full-sized and contained a sheet of paper on which he had written some lines of poetry.

> *But at my back I always hear*
> *Time's winged chariot hurrying near,*
> *And yonder all before us lie*
> *Deserts of vast eternity.*
> *Thy beauty shall no more be found,*
> *Nor, in thy marble vaults, shall sound*
> *My echoing song; then worms shall try*
> *That long-preserved virginity,*
> *And your quaint honour turn to dust,*
> *And into ashes all my lust:*
> *The grave's a fine and private place,*
> *But none, I think, do there embrace.*

Her reaction to this was to search her bag for coins for the telephone in the hallway. When Miss Howard came on the line, Annis said, 'Would you please impress on Mr Wolfe that I don't wish to receive any more presents from him.'

'Would you like to speak to him yourself, Miss Rossiter?'

'No, thank you. I have no desire to have any further contact with Mr Wolfe. I'm sure you can make that clear to him. Goodbye, Miss Howard.'

She rang off, hoping that when his amanuensis relayed the message to him, Drogo's annoyance at Miss Howard being privy to the brush-off would ensure that he wanted no further contact with Annis.

When a week passed and nothing more happened, it seemed that the telephone call had been effective. To some extent her life resumed its former tranquillity.

At times she was tempted to get rid of the azalea and the bay tree, tangible reminders of an episode she preferred to forget. But just as destroying the paper with the lines of poetry on it had not erased them from her mind, so the absence of the two plants would not make her forget Drogo's abominable behaviour the night she dined with him.

An early heat-wave made her long more than ever to own a place in the country where she could devote all her time to the work which she now knew to be her true métier. It was very frustrating to have time for it only in the evenings. But perhaps it wouldn't be too long before the estate agents reported that someone was interested in Morne Island.

While the fine weather lasted she spent her lunch hours sitting in the nearest park with her face turned up to the sun, regaining a little of the golden glow which had once been her all-year-round colour.

On the afternoon of the day when she should have met Drogo to hear his decision about the island, she was wrapping some cosmetics for a regular customer when she glanced up and was unnerved to see him inspecting the display at the other end of her section of the counter.

CHAPTER THREE

THE sight of him made her flush scarlet. Her fingers which, an instant before, had been accomplishing their task with practised deftness, became suddenly clusmy. Fortunately her customer was consulting a small black pocket diary, and did not notice these reactions.

'May I help you, sir?'

The question was addressed to Drogo by one of the other salesgirls.

'Thank you, but I want to have a word with your colleague when she's free,' was his reply.

Even if she had not already caught sight of him, Annis would have known who was speaking. Like that of certain actors and politicians, his voice had an unmistakable timbre. The sound of it sent a slow shiver through her. It rekindled the anger and chagrin which had followed their previous encounter and which, although not forgotten—to get over that humiliation would take months, if not years—had begun to lose some of its rawness.

The woman whom she had been serving said a smiling goodbye and departed, and her place across the glass counter with its lighted display of crystal flacons was taken by Drogo.

He was casually dressed in a blouson of soft, supple leather with raglan-style sleeves which showed the breadth of his shoulders just as the cut of his pants displayed the long lines of his thighs and the lean hips and flat, rock-hard midriff of a man who was all bone and muscle with none of the flabbiness Annis was accustomed to seeing on the store's wealthy customers.

'You have no right to pester me here,' she breathed, in a low irate voice.

Drogo ignored this remark. His manner very much that of any ordinary masculine customer, he said, 'Good afternoon. I want to buy a present for a friend who always uses this brand of cosmetics. Have any new products which she may not have tried been introduced recently?'

After a little hesitation, she indicated a large, satin-lined presentation coffret containing an ounce bottle of scent, *eau de toilette*, soap, body lotion and *bain moussant*, a perfumed foam bath.

'This is new,' she informed him stiffly. 'But the scent might not suit your friend's skin. It would be safer to give her one which she has used successfully—if you know the name of one of her favourites.'

'I don't, but I'm sure I should recognise the one which she often wears if you wouldn't mind spraying a little of each on your wrist for me to smell.'

His eyes held a gleam of mockery which seemed to confirm her suspicion that although there might be some substance in his claim to be seeking a present, he could easily have bought it elsewhere, and had chosen to come to where she worked from a cruel whim to test her reaction to seeing him again.

'What is your friend's colouring, sir? Is she fair, dark or auburn?' she asked him.

Drogo's firm mouth quirked at one corner, perhaps at the formal 'sir', or perhaps because his keen ear detected a slightly sarcastic inflection in her use of the word 'friend.'

'She's white-haired now, but she was a brunette,' he replied.

Annis hid her surprise at this answer. 'In that case we'd better enlist Miss Goodwin's help. Linda ...'

The dark-haired girl who had spoken to him earlier came from her part of the counter to stand beside Annis, her interest in Drogo as patent as Annis's pretended indifference to him.

'This gentleman doesn't know the name of the scent he wants to buy, but he thinks he may recognise the smell. As it's for someone with your colouring, would you mind if we tested it on you?'

'Not at all.' Clearly Linda was delighted to co-operate in the service of this tall, virile-looking customer.

She unbuttoned the cuff of her blouse and rolled back the sleeve, baring a rounded white forearm for Annis to spray with one of the several tester atomisers.

'It takes a few moments for the scent to develop,' Linda explained to him, with her most alluring, lash-fluttering smile.

'So I believe.'

In Drogo's answering smile Annis could read the certainty that in Linda, if he were interested, was yet another of the easy conquests to which he seemed to be accustomed.

When the other girl offered her arm to him, he cupped her hand in his palm and bent his dark head to the blue-veined skin at the wrist which had received the first spray.

'No, that isn't it,' he said, straightening, and letting go of Linda's hand.

Annis applied a second patch, and wondered if, had it been her hand, he would deliberately have held it while the second scent developed.

To Linda's visible disappointment, the second scent was one he recognised. She would have stayed with them until his purchase was completed, and Annis would have welcomed her presence, had not another customer approached the adjoining section of counter, obliging her to return there.

When she had gone, and Annis had been through the routine enquiries about whether he wished the coffret to be gift-wrapped, and would pay cash or wanted it charged, Drogo said, 'It seems you neglected to mention to the people who are handling the sale of Morne Island for you that there was one prospective buyer whose offer would not be acceptable. Or have you now changed your mind about not wishing to sell it to me?'.

She gave him a startled glance. 'They've offered it to you?'

'They're a leading firm with whom I've had many dealings. They're aware that, some time ago, I was actively looking for such a property. I suggest we discuss the matter over a drink when the store closes.' He named the bar of a nearby hotel. 'You'll be safe with me there,' he said blandly.

Without waiting for her reply, he picked up his parcel and strolled away.

'Did he charge it? Who was he?' asked Linda, as soon as she had finished attending to her customer.

'D. J. K. Wolfe,' answered Annis. At that moment it was her intention to go straight home, and let Drogo wait at the bar until his patience was exhausted.

'Wolf by nature as well as by name, I should think, wouldn't you?' said Linda, with a giggle. 'But I wouldn't mind being the girl he was shopping for. He must have plenty of money as well as being a dish. I'd have taken him for a foreigner, but he can't be with a name like that. Did you notice his hair? That kind of thick black curly hair really switches me on. Imagine burying your fingers in it—ooh!' Her exclamation was accompanied by a sensuous wriggle.

It was half an hour before closing time. Without any more customers to occupy her attention, Annis found it impossible not to think about Drogo, and to wonder if, by failing to attend the rendezvous he had proposed, she would be giving him a set-down at a cost to herself which far outweighed the satisfaction of snubbing his arrogance.

The more she thought about it, the harder it was to resist the chance of selling the island and thereby achieving her secret ambition. She was, she realised, becoming increasingly bored by her present job, and wasn't it Nietzsche, the German philosopher, who had said that life was a hundred times too short for people to allow themselves to be bored?

Drogo was not alone when she entered the opulent cocktail lounge. He was sitting in a secluded corner away from the bar where most of the tall stools were occupied, and with him was another man. They both rose as she approached, and Drogo introduced his companion as Stanley Berwick. They were of an age, but markedly different in all other respects. Mr Berwick had thinning hair and thick spectacles. His suit was a conservative grey chalk stripe, his shirt white, his tie grey and black. His handshake lacked strength, and his manner was oddly deferential. He struck Annis as an unlikely person for Drogo to associate with, but she welcomed his presence as an added safeguard against even a slight repetition of Drogo's outrageous behaviour at his apartment.

A waiter had noticed her arrival, and was hovering attentively when Drogo asked what she wished to drink.

'Nothing for me, thank you.' She wanted to emphasise that this wasn't a social occasion.

He spoke to the waiter in what sounded like Italian. The man smiled and bowed, and left them.

Annis seated herself on a reproduction French chair next to Mr Berwick's place on the right-angled sofa which filled that corner of the lounge. There she was facing Drogo, but securely separated from him by the other man.

'Berwick is a member of my legal staff,' Drogo explained. 'Although it's not usual for a buyer to have the vendor's interests at heart, in the case of Morne Island, I think you need to be made aware of the peculiar difficulties of your position.'

'The peculiar difficulties?' she echoed.

Drogo nodded to the other man, who turned to her and said in a grave tone, 'Are we correct in assuming that you have become permanently resident in this country, Miss Rossiter?'

'I've been living here for over a year, and I mean to remain here, if that's what you mean.'

He nodded. 'And you're paying income tax on your salary?'

'On my wages—yes. I'm given a weekly pay packet with the tax already deducted.'

His pale face took on an expression which made Annis feel she had mentioned something better left unsaid. 'The form of your remuneration is immaterial, Miss Rossiter. The salient factor is your tax liability which, unfortunately, now must include all your assets, both here and elsewhere.'

'The island is my only asset. How can an island be taxable? There's no income from it. The house isn't let to anyone. It's just standing empty.'

'What Berwick is getting at—and I brought him along in case you refused to believe me—is that, if you sell the island, a very large slice of the proceeds will end up in the

Treasury's coffers rather than yours,' explained Drogo. 'Show her your estimate, Berwick.'

The other man produced a paper on which were set out various figures which he proceeded to explain. 'These are only approximate, of course, but they do give some indication——'

He went on at some length while Annis digested the fact that even if Drogo were to pay the full price set by the agents, she would receive only a fraction of it.

'But this is monstrous,' she protested, when Stanley Berwick had finished speaking. 'Why should they take so much from me? It isn't fair. It isn't just.'

'A great many people would agree with you,' was Drogo's ironic comment. 'Particularly those owners of Britain's historic houses who have to sell paintings and furnishings—many of which go abroad—to keep their roofs watertight and their fabric in reasonable repair. However that is the system, and one must either accept it, or find ways to circumvent it.'

It was at this point that the waiter returned, and placed on the table in front of her a glass of a creamy golden liquid for which, momentarily forgetting that she had refused a drink, she gave him an absent-minded smile of thanks.

'Can I circumvent it?' she asked.

'I'm afraid not—not now, Miss Rossiter,' was Stanley Berwick's reply. 'There are methods of tax avoidance—which is quite a different thing from tax evasion, you understand—but they require careful forethought. Had your late parent transferred the property to you some years before his demise, or had you still been in residence there——'

'Yes, well he didn't, and she isn't, so it's more to the point to consider what can be done now, rather than what might have been done,' Drogo interrupted, in a brisk tone.

'But if Mr Berwick says there's no way——' Annis started.

She, too, did not finish her remark. 'On the contrary, there is one way in which we can both achieve our objectives,' he continued. 'But as Berwick has an engagement this evening, we need not detain him while I explain it to you. Off you go, Berwick. Goodnight.'

'Goodnight, sir. Goodnight, Miss Rossiter.' Leaving at least two inches of lager in his glass, he picked up his briefcase and hurried away.

'You might have let him finish his drink,' she objected.

Drogo shrugged. 'He could have done so.'

'What is this, which you ordered without consulting me?' she asked stiffly.

'It's called a Parson's Particular. There's no alcohol in it, only fruit juices and egg yolk. You'll find it refreshing— or so I'm told by my aunts. They restore themselves with it after an orgy of shopping.'

Somewhat reluctantly, Annis sipped it. 'As I also have an engagement this evening, perhaps you'd explain what you meant by there was one way to avoid losing all that money,' she said.

'You mentioned wanting a country cottage. I have one.' His posture and manner were as relaxed as hers were guarded.

'You're suggesting we should do a swop?' Before he could answer, she added, 'But as well as a cottage I need some money to live on while I——'

'While you what?' he prompted. 'Write a book?'

Her eyes widened. 'What makes you say that?'

'Both your parents were writers. It wouldn't be surprising if you had a similar bent. The thought did occur to me when you mentioned that some of your customers told you their life stories. I should think only a novelist or a psychiatrist would find such confidences interesting.'

'You're right, I do want to write. But not fiction. Facts are my line. The historical facts which were my mother's speciality.'

'In that case my proposal should suit you admirably. It would give you the time and the means to do all the research you desired.'

'What is your proposal?' she asked.

'The usual kind of proposal between a man and a woman —as distinct from a proposition. In effect, I put that to you last time. Tonight my intentions are wholly honourable. I'm suggesting we should marry. That way we can each do what's supposed to be impossible—have our cake and eat it.'

Later Annis wondered for how long she had sat staring at him in transfixed disbelief that she could have heard him aright.

After some seconds, or minutes, Drogo spoke again. 'You think I'm not serious? I am. Never more so.'

'How can you be?' she expostulated. 'Why, we ... we scarcely know each other!'

'In many marriages, the couple still don't really know each other after living together for twenty years,' was his dry response. 'You and I know all that's necessary at the outset of a relationship. You know that I can provide for you, and that being my wife won't conflict with your literary inclinations. I know I shall be your first lover.'

'Is that important to you?' she said, in surprise.

She knew that virginity had mattered to her parents' generation, and mattered still in countries where women continued to be men's chattels. But since coming to Europe she had formed the impression that it was of little or no account in the Western world where men and women were now on an equal footing; and certainly Drogo was the last person she would have expected to attach any importance to it.

He answered her question by saying, 'It hasn't been, in the past. But now that the time has come to settle down and found my dynasty, I find I have an atavistic desire for an old-fashioned bride who's not been in other men's beds.'

'And love—is that *un*important?'

'There again my views are not in line with contemporary thought. I believe that if a couple choose each other for the sound, unemotional reasons which were the basis of unions arranged by parents, they stand an excellent chance of being very happy together. Don't you feel you could be happy as my wife?'

'I've never given it a thought. Why should I, when last time we met you seemed bent on depriving me of the very thing which now appears to be my principal value to you?'

'Oh, not your principal value.' His hazel eyes raked her figure. 'I'm not sure which I'd rate highest—your beauty or your intelligence. I'd put them coequally, probably, for I certainly shouldn't want you for my wife if you were a dumb blonde, or a bluestocking with a plain face.'

'I suppose you think I should be flattered that I seem to come up to your standards,' she retorted acidly. 'In fact I'm amazed; amazed by your incredible arrogance in assuming that because I fulfil your requirements, you're bound to meet mine. I'm sorry to tell you that you don't—not by a long chalk.'

But this thrust, which she hoped would annoy him, seemed only to cause him amusement.

'In what way do I fall short? Not financially, at any rate.'

'No, one couldn't fault you on that score,' Annis conceded. 'But there are some women, you know, for whom a man's financial standing is of less account than his personal qualities.'

'If there are, I have yet to meet one,' Drogo said smoothly. 'And frankly I think any woman who disregarded *my* financial standing would be extraordinarily stupid. As I think I told you before, all the best things in life are not free. The rain may fall on the just and the unjust, but it falls a lot less on the rich than it does on the poor because the rich can afford to escape to the sun when they've had too much of the wet. Don't tell me you wouldn't like to go back to Morne Island sometimes. I shan't believe you.'

'I should ... I should love to go back. But not at *any* price,' she answered.

He leaned towards her, his strange tawny eyes fixing and holding her gaze so that she found it impossible to look away.

'I'm not an old man,' he said mildly. 'Nor did you appear to find my kisses unpleasant before you felt bound to resist them. Would bearing my children be such a high price to pay for a life of unlimited luxury? You would have no domestic duties except those you chose to assume. You'd be free in a way which few people are—freer than I am myself. Total freedom to do as one pleases is not something to be rejected lightly, my dear Annis.'

His words conjured for her a vision of a life of untrammelled indulgence in all the things she liked best; long hours of undisturbed reading, the time to explore all the lesser-known corners of London, the means to travel to the places where the history she was writing had been made, and in the cosseted comfort of a VIP's wife, not as one of the economy-class herd.

'I—I just can't believe you can be s-serious,' she stammered.

'Do you really have an engagement this evening?' he enquired, his mouth quirking slightly.

She flushed, and admitted she hadn't.

'Then we'll dine here—safely in public—and I'll strive to convince you,' was his answer. 'Will you excuse me for a few minutes while I make a telephone call?'

'Of course.'

Annis welcomed the respite from his presence in which to pull herself together. How long had this incredible suggestion been in his mind? she wondered, as she watched him stride away. When she reached for the glass to drink some more of the fruit cocktail, it surprised her that her hand was quite steady in spite of the shock she had undergone.

She picked up the sheet of paper, and scanned again the calculations of how little would be left to her from the sale of the island. She had never given much thought to the rights and wrongs of inherited wealth and property, but now she burned with resentment that so large a share of her patrimony could be taken away from her.

A woman walked into the bar dressed in scarlet silk crêpe-de-chine, with a blue fox jacket slung carelessly over her shoulders, and a diamond on a platinum chain sparkling in the hollow at the base of her throat.

As his wife, I could dress like that, Annis thought; and she could not deny she was tempted by the thought of the exquisite clothes and the fabulous jewels she could wear if she were to accept Drogo's amazing proposal.

It was not, as he had pointed out, as if he were old and repulsive to her. He was as virile and charming as any man she had met. But he didn't love her, or she him; and she had grown up believing in romantic love as strongly as earlier generations had believed in heaven.

Supposing she were to marry him, and then meet the love of her life? And supposing the love of her life turned out to be a poor man who couldn't afford to support her unaided, and needed her to contribute to repaying the mortgage on a house or a flat in the endless sprawl of Greater London where girls like Linda Goodwin lived before they were married and afterwards? Not for them a huge penthouse apartment with its own swimming pool. Not for them the leisure and money to follow their own inclinations.

The lives of most women were governed by the needs of their husbands and children; the unremitting daily discipline of cleaning and cooking, and generally making ends meet. Did love compensate for the sacrifice of youthful ambitions and daydreams?

As these thoughts whirled through her mind, she saw him returning from his call, and noticed the woman in red turning bored eyes in his direction, eyes which ceased to be bored as they took in his tall, erect figure and the authority of his bearing. Watching her as she watched Drogo made Annis realise there must be many women in London who would think her mad even to hesitate before accepting his proposal.

As before, when she had dined alone with him, he proved an agreeable companion. Afterwards, he put her into a taxi, saying, 'Tomorrow I'm off to Singapore. I'll give you till next Monday night to make up your mind. Meet me here at the same time, will you? Goodnight, Annis.'

He kissed her hand, and shut the door. Then he gave some money to the driver and told the man where to take her. She last saw him walking away in the opposite direction.

When, about ten minutes later, she unlocked the door of her room and felt for the light switch, she knew she was far too strung up to go straight to bed, or to concentrate on the work with which her evenings were normally occupied.

Her kitchen consisted of a sink unit and a baby cooker hidden from view by a screen covered with such hideous material that after a fortnight she had been unable to live with it any longer, and had pinned on a covering of cheap brown and white gingham which did not offend her eye every time she looked in that direction.

Before taking off her outdoor clothes, she lit the gas and put on a kettle to make herself a pot of tea. She did not particularly like tea, but it was preferable to instant coffee. As she reached for the box of tea-bags, it struck her that, as Drogo's wife, she would be able always to drink real coffee.

The room had a central table, and a smaller one against the wall where she worked on her nightly task. When, during her visit to his flat, Drogo had asked if there was a man in her life, and she had implied that there was, and that she had made his acquaintance in a junk shop, there had been some truth in her answer. But the man who, for some time, had occupied her evenings to the exclusion of all others was not a living man; he had been dead for more than a century, having lived to a great age after distinguishing himself in England's battles against Napoleon.

He had become known to Annis through his letters, a parcel of which she had bought for less than a pound. It had taken her weeks to decipher them. Not only had the ink faded but, in the manner of many letter-writers in his day, the General had not only crossed the paper from side to side but had written another set of lines, the rows running from top to bottom.

But, having painstakingly unravelled the jumble of words, and copied them out in her own clear hand, Annis had realised that here was the nucleus of the life of an outstanding man who, perhaps because he had no descendants to keep his memory green, had escaped the notice of historians. To Annis, being her mother's daughter, this had been as exciting as finding the ore which held gold.

However, by now her work on him had reached the stage when she could not progress without spending hours in public and regimental archives, and this was virtually impossible as long as she worked at the store.

But if she were Drogo's wife, her research could gallop instead of progressing at a crawl, as it was at present.

She remembered her father had been fond of quoting Thomas Carlyle. *Blessed is he who has found his work; let him ask no other blessedness.*

She had found her work. Marriage to Drogo would not only give her freedom to pursue it, but entitle her to many other blessings. Surely she would be mad to refuse him?

When Annis gave Drogo her answer, he produced from his pocket a magnificent starburst of diamonds.

'You were very sure I'd say yes,' she commented.

He smiled at her. 'Reasonably sure.'

When it came to planing the wedding, which he wanted to take place as soon as possible, she would have settled for the brief formalities of a register office, a dress which she could wear again on other occasions, and perhaps a small luncheon party for Drogo's aunts and the Bairds and, on her side, old Mrs Leveson.

He, however, had other ideas.

'No, no—that won't do,' he said, dismissing her suggestions. 'You've already missed most of the pleasures of a normal girlhood. At least you shall have a proper wedding to look back on. I've been to a number of civil marriages, and I don't think you'd like the businesslike atmosphere. Even though we're not normally churchgoers, I see no reason why we shouldn't be married in the traditional manner.'

'Isn't it hypocritical to make vows before a God you don't believe in?' she suggested.

'Perhaps, but at least there will be no hypocrisy in your wearing a white dress,' he answered dryly.

So she found herself swept along by the preparations for a large, lavish ceremony to be attended by all Drogo's friends and associates. But very few responsibilities devolved upon her. The rôle which, normally, would have been played by her mother was borne, with professional expertise, by a well-bred widow who had made a profession of organising functions, and in whose competent hands everything progressed without a hitch.

'I always dress at Hardy Amies,' said this person, when Annis asked her advice about a wedding dress. 'If you like, I could introduce you.'

Annis had often gazed admiringly at the clothes displayed in the famous couturier's ready-to-wear shop near Harrods. But even his off-the-peg designs had been far above her touch. Now, as if in a dream, she found herself being measured for a white silk taffeta bridal gown in his couture house in Savile Row, the street world-famous for the perfection of its tailoring for men.

During this time, as well as paying for her trousseau, Drogo lavished presents upon her. At first she protested;

later she began to accept that it pleased him to shower her with luxurious luggage from Gucci, pretty trifles from Cartier and anything else which caught his eye in the shop windows of Old Bond Street.

He would have removed her from her bedsitter, and installed her in a good hotel, but at this she dug her heels in, insisting on remaining where she was even after she had finished working at the store.

One thing he did not do was to introduce her to his friends. When she mentioned this, Drogo said there would be plenty of time for that later. For the present he seemed to prefer to keep her to himself, although once or twice he invited the Bairds to make up a party to go to the theatre.

One day, having lunch with Diana, Annis said, 'I don't think you really approve of this marriage, do you?'

Diana looked at first startled and then somewhat embarrassed. After a few moments' hesitation, she answered, 'I don't disapprove of it, Annis. I do wonder if you aren't rather young to commit yourself to a relationship which is supposed to be for life. I know many of your generation no longer see it in those terms. They aren't worried by the prospect of a divorce if a marriage doesn't work out. But any sort of failure leaves scars, and I'm sure the failure of a marriage must be terribly hurtful to any sensitive person. I think under your self-contained manner, you're even more vulnerable than most young girls. Are you wildly in love with Drogo? You don't show it, but I suppose you must be?'

It was Annis' turn to hesitate. Then, impelled by a need to tell the truth, even if Diana were shocked by it, she said, 'No, it isn't a love match on either side. It's a marriage of mutual convenience.'

'Oh, but——' Diana stopped short, looking puzzled

rather than shocked. 'But surely you must love him ... a little,' she began again, after a pause. 'He's so attractive ... so compelling. Most women can't resist him, and although *he* may say that it's only because of his money, obviously it isn't. How can you *not* love him, Annis?'

'I do find him extremely attractive,' Annis acknowledged. 'But that isn't the same as being wildly in love, as you put it. I don't know that I'm even capable of feeling that desperate emotion. Probably not. When Lord Byron wrote that love was "a thing apart" for men, but "women's whole existence", don't you think he could have been misled by the fact that the women of his day, although often very highly educated, had so little scope for their abilities? Now, when there's masses of scope, love's a thing apart for us, too. Not for all women perhaps. It's obvious that you adore David, and are completely fulfilled by making him happy and comfortable.'

'Yes—yes, I am,' agreed the older woman. 'I was never much enthused by the job I had before our marriage. Becoming his wife, and my own mistress, was as much a release for me as retirement is for most men. I've never ceased to feel pleased that I don't have to go *out* to work, but can do it at home, in my own time and in my own way.'

Annis nodded. 'I shall feel something like that myself. I shan't be involved in domestic doings, but I shall become my own mistress instead of a wage-slave.'

'Even though you won't have any actual housework to do, I expect you'll soon find yourself involved in all the other activities which occupy the wives of men like Drogo. Fund-raising committees, and so forth.'

'Oh, no, I shan't do that, Diana. I mean to write—like my parents.'

'Does Drogo know this?' asked Diana.

'Of course. He has no objection. Why should he have?'

'Well, no—if it's just a hobby and doesn't conflict with his interests.'

'It will be much more than a hobby. I mean to work all day and every day. Not for quite the same hours as I did at the store, probably from ten o'clock to four o'clock.'

'When you're here in London, and Drogo is busy—yes, possibly. I can see that it may be a good thing for you to have your own interests. But I don't think you'll find him too tolerant of anything you want to do when he wants to do something else. And, being rather older than you, I expect he'll want you to start having children immediately. Have you talked about that with him, Annis? It's important to discuss it, and make sure you both share the same ideas on the subject.'

'Yes, I know he's keen to have children. But they won't stop me working,' said Annis. 'There'll be a nanny to cope with the napkins and bottles. I shall only have the pleasant side of motherhood ... playing with them ... reading their bedtime stories.'

'Oh, there'll be no problems as long as they're little. Drogo will treat them like puppies, and they'll think he's a hero. The difficulties will come later on when they're growing up and you have to keep the peace between several rebellious teenagers and a somewhat overbearing father. For Drogo can be overbearing, make no mistake about that.'

'I discovered it ages ago,' said Annis, with a rueful smile. 'But all the problems you're raising are in the far distant future. I expect I shall cope when the time comes. Is that your only dubiety about us, Diana?—That I'm ten years his junior?'

Mrs Baird looked thoughtfully at her. 'I'm not sure I know what to think, now you tell me you aren't deeply in love with him. Love has its perils, goodness knows, but to marry without it seems equally dangerous. Even the happiest marriage has its periods of discord, you know. I just don't believe those couples who claim they never have a row.'

'I don't recall my parents having a row,' Annis said reflectively. 'But perhaps, if they ever had cross words, they saved them till after my bedtime. And as my father was already middle-aged, and my mother in her thirties, when they married, I daresay they were much more tolerant than a young couple learning to live together.'

'Yes, probably—and no doubt your experience of living alone on that island with an elderly father will prove to have been useful practice for living with a younger but equally dominating husband,' was Diana's reply.

One weekend Drogo took her to see the country cottage he had mentioned on the night of his proposal. It was actually a row of cottages which had been knocked into one and done up far more attractively and comfortably than anything Annis had visualised buying on her own account.

A woman from the nearby village looked after the place, and cooked them an excellent lunch, after which they drove on to visit the two women who, since the death of his father, had become his closest relations on his English side.

Drogo's aunts had been girls of nineteen and seventeen at the outbreak of the second world war, and were now on the brink of their sixties. The elder of the two, his Aunt Freddy—short for Frederica—had been widowed twice during the war years. Perhaps because of her sister's experience, his Aunt Tessa, although very pretty, had never married at all.

'Although I don't think she would qualify as a spinster in the usual sense of the word,' Drogo had added, while telling Annis something about them on the way.

Having no need to work to support themselves, after the war the two women had set up house together. Aunt Freddy had taken up gardening and was now an authority on herbs, while Aunt Tessa had gone through a gamut of interests, and was now adept at almost every type of handcraft.

Based on Drogo's brief thumbnail sketches, Annis's pre-conception of them was of two faded, grey-haired women, probably dressed in homespuns woven by Tessa. This picture was instantly dispelled when they found Frederica Ford clipping the hedge between her garden and the country lane on which she lived, looking, when seen from behind, no older than Anni.. The only grey thing about her was the colour of her needlecord bib-and-brace worn over a scarlet pole matched by the lacquered nails on the smooth, well-kept hand she withdrew from her gardening glove before she held it out to her visitor.

Her sister, whom they found tossing a salad in the kitchen, was equally unlike Annis's idea of a woman who baked and bottled and had her own electric kiln. At fifty-eight, Tessa Wolfe was still a lovely woman with an almost unlined complexion, and large eyes skilfully made up to enhance the deep blue of her irises.

As Annis had anticipated, they both adored their tall nephew, but it seemed to be an unpossessive affection which did not make them critical of her. Long before supper was over she had relaxed in the warmth of their friendliness.

As the cottage had only three bedrooms, Drogo was

spending the night in a room at the local pub where the landlady did bed and breakfast. At the end of the evening, when it was time for him to go to the village, he gave Annis a brief goodnight kiss in the presence of his aunts, but did not suggest that she should walk as far as the gate with him or find any other excuse for a more prolonged embrace.

Under a green and white duvet on the double bed in the visitors' room, Annis slept more soundly than she had for a long time. She was woken by Tessa bringing her tea and biscuits on a small round acrylic tray patterned with lilies of the valley like the bedroom wallpaper.

'May I stay and talk, or do you detest chatter before breakfast?' Miss Wolfe asked.

Although wrapped in a geranium-pink cotton velours robe, she had already made up her face and smelled deliciously of *Cinnabar*.

'No, no—please do stay,' answered Annis. 'I slept like a top, thank you. This is a most comfortable bed'—in reply to Tessa's next question.

'Did Drogo sleep at the White Hart out of respect for our sensibilities, or yours?' was his younger aunt's third one.

'For mine,' said Annis, colouring slightly.

'You must be exceptionally strong-minded if you've kept him at bay all this time,' was Tessa's comment. 'Even in our youth it wasn't unusual for engaged couples to sleep together whenever they could. Not with the approval of their elders, of course, but they managed it nevertheless.'

Annis lifted the quilted green cosy from the one-person teapot. 'I can understand that, during the war, when everyone's future was so uncertain.'

'That was partly the reason, of course. It was certainly

a favourite masculine argument against us resisting our instincts. Mind you, instincts can be misleading: they can make you think yourself in love with the most unsuitable people. Mine certainly did. Had I married the first man who ever made love to me, I shouldn't have been at all happy, because we had nothing else in common, and he wasn't even a good lover,' Tessa added candidly.

Annis filled the fine china tea-cup. 'I don't think I need worry about Drogo's prowess. He seems to have had plenty of practice.'

'His chequered past doesn't bother you?'

'I don't feel it has anything to do with me.'

'Wise girl. It hasn't,' said Tessa. 'Nor does it indicate anything about his future. I've always felt that Drogo is very like my brother who, once he was married, never so much as glanced at another woman—at least not in an amorous way. Because she wasn't a beauty, although she dressed with great flair, unkind people used to murmur that he'd married my sister-in-law for her money—her father's money. But that wasn't the case. It was a genuine love match which lasted until they were killed.'

'When did that happen?' asked Annis. 'Drogo never speaks of them.'

'No, he wouldn't. If anyone mentions them, he becomes very clipped and withdrawn. The memory of his parents is still a raw spot. Their loss might have been less painful for him had he had some brothers and sisters. But my sister-in-law was unable to have any more children—a great disappointment, particularly as she, too, was an only child, and her father had hoped for several grandsons. The old man was rather a terror and, after their death, he became the dominant force in Drogo's life from the age of eight until he was in his late teens. To understand Drogo in his

difficult moods—not that we ever see them, but others do—
you need to appreciate that, after an extremely happy
early life, he went through a period of quite tyrannical
bullying which would have broken most boys. Drogo refused to be broken, and standing up to his grandfather
forged a hard core of toughness in him, and a certain impatience and intolerance of weakness in others. If you
understand that, you're halfway to understanding——'

A tap at the door made her break off. 'That must be
him. Freddy is out on her early morning walk and won't
be back for half an hour yet. Come in, Drogo.'

The room was under the eaves, with a narrow staircase
winding up to a low cottage door which forced Drogo to
duck his head before he could enter.

'Good morning.' He smiled at his aunt who was sitting
in a chair by the window. Then he turned to look towards
the bed where Annis was leaning against the padded cotton-
covered headboard. 'Good morning,' he repeated.

'Good morning.' She made an instinctive movement to
pull up the sheet, forgetting that on this bed there was no
top sheet, only the cover of the duvet which she could not
manage with one hand without the risk of a spill.

'Has Mrs Murphy given you breakfast already, Drogo?'
asked his aunt, on a note of surprise.

'No, I told her that on this occasion I'd forgo her excellent Irish breakfast and have something here,' he explained.
'But I'm not particularly hungry. I can wait until Freddy
comes back.'

'At least have a cup of coffee. I left the pot perking
gently. I'll get you one. Have this chair,' suggested Miss
Wolfe, as she stood up.

However, as she went downstairs, Drogo did not take
her place but came to the bedside, the only part of the

room where a man of his size could stand at full height and still have some clearance between his head and the ceiling.

This, and the fact that the bedroom was more feminine than masculine in the style of its decor, made him seem even more tall and male than he did in the rest of the house. Annis's nightdress was not a filmy one. She disliked the slithery feel of synthetic materials against her skin, and preferred to wear lightweight cottons such as her present garment, a cucumber-green and white print from the Laura Ashley Bargain Shop where she picked up a lot of her house clothes. But although the nightgown was not transparent, the shirring had slackened in the wash and it would be all too easy to slip off her shoulders.

How long would it be before his aunt returned? she wondered uneasily, as Drogo seated himself beside her, and she saw the hot light of desire flame in his eyes as he looked at her.

'I like you with your hair tousled. Let's remove this, and say good morning properly, shall we?'—taking the tray and, there being no space for it on the night-table, putting it down on the floor.

'Oh, no—I haven't brushed my teeth yet,' she protested, averting her face as he reached for her.

Drogo took a firm hold of her chin and turned her face round to his, ignoring her second 'No ... please,' and stifling a third objection with a hearty kiss to which she was forced to yield for as long as he chose to prolong it. At last he released her mouth and said, with his lips to her cheek, 'You taste as sweet as an apple. Don't tense. Why are you so nervous? My aunt will be back in a moment. There isn't time for me to do anything wicked to you.'

He drew back to look at her face, the skin round his

tawny eyes crinkling as he studied her flushed confusion. 'My God, but I'm going to enjoy having you in my bed!' he told her, with a kind of fierce relish.

Then the hand which had been under her chin slid round to grip her by the hair and pull her head back—not ungently as long as she submitted—exposing the line of her throat to his exploring lips which slowly worked their way downwards towards the frilled edge of the cotton above the wide band of shirring. This, he was already discovering, made it easy for him to pull down the front of her nightgown and extend the field for his kisses.

Annis foiled his intention by choosing to suffer the pain of jerking her head up; and when she did this he released both his hold on her hair and on the elasticated border which he had been in the act of stretching.

'I . . . your hand is cold,' she muttered, prompted by an obscure wish to justify her unwillingness.

There was some truth in the excuse. To anyone still partially cocooned in the warmth of the down-filled duvet his skin had an outdoor freshness which did feel cool at first contact. But that was not really the reason for her reluctance; nor was it the fact that his aunt had left the bedroom door open, and would soon rejoin them. At rock bottom, Annis knew, it was because she was afraid of this man who would soon be her husband; afraid that, in giving her freedom in some ways, he would enslave her in others, and she would find herself in a cage even more inescapable than her duty to her father.

Why this fear grew much stronger when Drogo was kissing her and touching her, she could not tell. But it was so. Always, when he kissed her, or even looked at her in a certain way, she had the nightmare sense of being on the brink of a trap from which, once it closed upon her, there would be no release, ever.

Drogo grasped the duvet with both hands and drew it higher until it was under her chin. He held it there, smiling, a slightly cruel glint in his eyes.

'Only ten days more, my dear Annis, and then we shall see if I'm mistaken in my reading of your innermost nature.'

'W-what do you mean by that?' she faltered.

'I mean that I expect and hope to find fire under the ice of your present primness.'

'And if you're disappointed?'

'I shan't be,' he answered confidently, removing himself to the chair and remaining at that safe distance until, a few minutes later, his aunt reappeared with the promised mug of coffee.

It was not until after lunch that he and Annis returned to London. For much of the way they listened to an orchestral concert. When the programme ended, Drogo switched off the radio and asked, 'What did you make of the aunts?'

'They were charming to me. I liked them. Do you think they approved of me?'

'I know it. Aunt Freddy told me they both thought I'd made an excellent choice.'

'I hope you have,' Annis answered, rather uncertainly, for it seemed to her that all the advantages of the match were on her side.

If she failed to satisfy his puzzling animal passion for her, and to give him the children he wanted, he would have made a bad bargain for which he might punish her by showing the difficult side which his aunt had said was the result of his youthful conflicts with his grandfather.

A few days before their wedding, after taking her to the theatre, Drogo invited himself up to her flatlet for a nightcap, and Annis did not demur.

In the main, his behaviour since their engagement had been surprisingly circumspect, causing her, if not to relax completely with him, at least to be less on her guard.

Thus it was that when, having drunk the coffee she had made for them, he rose from his chair and beckoned her to him, she expected a goodnight embrace of the unexceptionable kind to which he had restricted himself since placing the ring on her finger.

And this, at the beginning, it was. He put his arms loosely around her, and kissed the tapering curves of her eyebrows and the tip of her nose. Annis felt no inward recoil when his lips pressed lightly on hers. She no longer feared being seduced, as she had before their engagement. She assumed that now he would wait until after their marriage before he repeated the caresses he had inflicted upon her the first time she went to his apartment.

However, in this she was wrong. Instead of one short goodnight kiss, tonight his mouth lingered on hers, coaxing her closed lips to soften, and her hands, of their own volition, to slide up the wall of his chest and over his shoulders to meet at the back of his neck.

He bent forward, swaying her backwards and making her cling as if to a perilous overhang from which to lose hold would be to plunge into an abyss.

As his kisses grew fiercer and more devouring, she was scarcely aware of his warm hands untucking her shirt from the wide velvet belt of her skirt. Having pulled free the silky material, they slipped underneath it to fondle the curve of her waist, and there they remained for some minutes before sliding gradually higher to find the clip of her bra which, this time, was at the back.

'No, Drogo, don't,' she begged him.

'My dear girl, in less than a week we're going to be married.'

'I know, and then you can do whatever you please to me. But not until then—please, not yet.'

'Isn't that being rather excessively puritan?'

'Yes, perhaps it is, but I'd rather wait till we're married. It will spoil our wedding day for me if you ... undress me tonight.'

'I should like to do more than undress you,' he murmured, not letting her go when she tried to pull free of his arms. 'It might spoil our wedding day for you; it could only improve our wedding night. In love, as in most other things, a little practice is necessary before perfection is achieved. Isn't the start of our private life more important than the public show?'

All the time he was speaking, his lips were exploring her face and his hands were stroking her body, making nonsense of her protests that she didn't want him to make love to her.

She found herself torn between resistance and submission, as if she were two girls in one. When Drogo swung her up against his chest and carried her to the studio couch the submissive side of her thrilled to his masterful strength and to his experience as a lover.

But when, after several more kisses, she felt his hand on her knee, and then on her thigh—she was wearing fine stockings with seams rather than workaday tights—and then on her bare upper thigh, her resistance revived, and she struggled up, out of his arms.

'No, I won't be seduced in bedsit-land! I want my first night of love to be romantic ... in Paris,' she declared, trying to treat it lightly. 'Please go home now, Drogo.'

If, then, he had kissed her again, and repeated the slow,

gentle glide of his hand from her knee to her thigh, she would have succumbed to the aching longing of her senses, no matter what the surroundings. It was the man, not the place, who made a woman remember the first time with joy or regret.

As she jumped up and tucked in her shirt, she half wished he would persist, and she felt sure he knew it; and that when he got up to go, it was really his decision, not hers.

'Very well, if it's so important to you to remain a virgin until I've paid the bride-price—in this case marriage,' Drogo said mockingly.

He himself remained undishevelled, for his thick, curly, black Greek hair never looked untidy, and his clothes, being the best obtainable in a city renowned for men's clothes, never seemed to crumple or crease.

'You make it sound horrid—as if I were bartering myself. It isn't like that. If . . . if you were going to be executed, or fighting a war, or in danger of death in some way, then I should let you stay here tonight.'

He patted her cheek. 'Would you, Annis?'

It seemed to her now that she saw something else in his eyes, but it was one of several expressions which she always found hard to interpret with any certainty.

'Yes, I would. But it doesn't apply. So I'd rather that we said goodnight—until Wednesday.'

'So be it. Until Wednesday.' His expression was quizzical again.

Yet when he had gone she could almost but not quite convince herself that her rather foolish avowal had caused him to feel a momentary tenderness for her. And what she said had been true: if their future was somehow at risk, she would not have sent him away.

Because of her old-fashioned, isolated upbringing, she

found it hard to adapt to the freer code of her contemporaries. But this didn't mean her emotions were tepid, and self-control was easier for her. After Drogo had gone, and she was in bed on her own, she found herself longing for Wednesday as keenly as if she loved him and he loved her.

Early on the morning of her wedding day, Annis finished packing up her remaining belongings and left them with her elderly neighbour, to be fetched by Theron later on. Her going away clothes were hanging in Drogo's apartment, with certain items of her trousseau which Rosie would pack at the last moment.

Having locked her bedsitter and left the key and her rent-book with old Mrs Leveson, whom Theron would bring to the church as one of her half dozen guests, Annis took a taxi to the Bairds' flat.

As she had not wanted to be given away by Cousin Margaret's husband—but had felt obliged to invite them to the wedding—this office was being performed for her by David Baird.

At the flat she had a leisurely bath, and then a stylist from Aldo Bruno—one of London's most elegant hair salons—arrived to put up her hair with the six diamond-flower combs which had belonged to Drogo's mother. As the stylist finished, the fitter arrived with her wedding dress.

The marriage was taking place at St Margaret's, Westminster, the parish church of the House of Commons, and the church where all the most fashionable weddings were celebrated.

Although Annis was having no bridesmaids, they had had a rehearsal of the ceremony, and she knew that although the church dated from 1523, it had a simplicity which made it seem curiously modern.

The stained glass in the west window had a pattern like falling rain. The famous east window, made in Holland in 1505, depicted the betrothal of Catherine of Aragon to Prince Arthur, the brother of Henry the Eighth. Samuel Pepys had been married at St Margaret's, and Milton and Winston Churchill, and a long list of English aristocrats. The remains of Sir Walter Raleigh lay under the chancel.

A crowd of sightseers were awaiting her arrival as the car drew up outside the church, and David stepped out and turned to help her alight. She heard gasps of awed admiration as the women saw her lovely dress and the diamonds glittering on her veiled head.

. The church, almost empty at the rehearsal, was now full of guests, most of them strangers to her. Walking up the aisle on David's arm, she was vaguely aware of a battery of stares focused on her.

She had eyes for no one but Drogo who, wearing a grey morning coat with a slightly paler grey waistcoat and a crimson carnation in his buttonhole, had turned to watch her come towards him.

The service passed like a dream, and later she found she could only remember parts of it: repeating the vows, and seeing Drogo's lean hands take hold of her left one and slip the gold ring on her finger.

He had had it made specially for her by Andrew Grima, the most brilliant of modern English goldsmiths, and it paired with her Grima engagement ring so that when they were worn together the two rings merged into one.

When they emerged from the church, the crowd had increased and news photographers and a television cameraman, his camera balanced on his shoulder, were waiting to take pictures of them.

Annis flinched as the flashbulbs exploded, and Drogo looked down at her, smiling, and pressed her arm to his side in a gesture of protective encouragement.

Suddenly, like the startling flare of the flashes, she felt an explosive uprush of happiness. A radiant smile lit her face, making Drogo's tawny eyes gleam as he murmured, 'My beautiful wife!'

They walked to their car through a chorus of shouted good wishes.

As Annis's parents were dead, and Drogo did not wish to have the reception at his apartment, it was held in a suite of rooms owned by a firm of professional caterers, but having the appointments and atmosphere of a rather grand private town house.

Drogo had been there often, attending other people's weddings. He told her there was a bride's room where, very often, they changed into their going away clothes preparatory to setting out on their honeymoon journey.

Because, for the time being, they were to have only a short honeymoon in Paris, with a longer visit to the West Indies later on, when Drogo had fewer commitments which it was inconvenient to cancel or postpone, it had been arranged that Annis should change at the apartment where they could relax for an hour or two between leaving the reception and flying to France.

Alone in the bride's room, she changed her engagement ring from her right hand back to her left one, retouched her lips and refreshed her light, floral scent, and then returned to the public rooms where Drogo had been joined by the Bairds, and by his best man and his wife, John and Melissa.

Annis had met them—they had come down from their home in the Highlands for one night only—at a luncheon party at the apartment the day before. At night they had gone to the theatre, but she and Drogo had not accompanied them, nor had he arranged the traditional stag party. She had heard him tell John and David that he had no inclination to spend his last night as a bachelor in that sort of revelry, and as he had been to the play which John and Melissa wanted to see, he hoped they wouldn't mind if he followed the example of his bride-to-be and had an evening at home and an early night.

He had already said the same thing to Annis, explaining that being on their own was a rare treat for them nowadays. Having a farm and six children, three under school age, they could seldom get away together, and indeed must fly back to Scotland immediately after the reception.

It was not long before the rest of the guests began to arrive. As there were several hundred of them, Annis was glad he had decided they would not receive formally, shaking hands with everyone, but would merely circulate, speaking to those he particularly wished her to meet.

Even this was fairly taxing as, naturally, everyone was far more curious about her than if she had been one of themselves, the daughter of another rich man with a conventional background of boarding and finishing school. The only guests she could greet with genuine warmth were old Mrs Leveson and three of her fellow salesgirls.

At Drogo's insistence she drank some champagne, and swallowed some bite-size pieces of hot Croque Monsieur. But apart from the fact that she wasn't hungry, it was difficult to eat more than a few mouthfuls while responding to people's praise for her dress and good wishes for their future.

She was glad when at last Drogo murmured, 'I think we can leave very soon now.'

'I must just go back to the bride's room. I left my bag there.'

This was a small white silk bag containing a few make-up things which had been in the back of their car when they came out of church where the only thing she had carried had been a small spray of white orchids.

'Can't Diana fetch it for you?'

'I can't see her. I shan't be a minute.' She left him, and made her way to the curtain-draped archway which led to the bride's room.

She sensed that Drogo had had enough ceremonial for one day, so she was as quick as she could be. Even so, when she returned, there had been some slight changes among the groups eating and chatting, and now there was a couple of women in low-toned conversation near the archway.

They both had their backs to her and, before she could murmur, 'Would you excuse me?' she heard one of them say:

'I never took Drogo for a saint, but I shouldn't have thought even he would have the gall to spend the night before his wedding with his mistress.'

'He didn't! How do you know?' The second voice sounded gleeful rather than shocked.

'I've a friend who lives in the same block of flats as Fiona. Hermione and her husband don't know Drogo, except by sight, but she's seen him arriving and leaving a number of times. Last night, coming home from a dinner party, they met him stepping out of the lift. As it was after one in the morning, they assumed—as who wouldn't?— that a fond farewell had been taking place. Only a temporary one, probably. I daresay it won't be too long after the honeymoon before he revisits the love-nest. This girl he has married is lovely, but so young and not very animated. They say that Fiona's the wittiest woman in London, and such hot stuff in bed that——'

But this was the last Annis heard as she fled to the room she had left, and the unknown speaker went on with her salacious gossip, unaware of the shattering blow she had dealt to the bride described in one morning newspaper as 'the most envied girl of the year.'

CHAPTER FOUR

THE changing room door had a small sliding bolt above the handle. Annis bolted the door and sank into the nearest chair, careless of crushing her full skirts, her mind reeling from the shock of what she had overheard.

She had known from the first that there must have been many women before her in Drogo's life. But somehow she had formed the impression during their engagement that, for the present and at least in the immediate future, there was no one but herself.

The possibility—no, more than that, the likelihood—that she would not always be able to hold him was something she had faced and accepted. But this discovery that, ever since she had accepted his proposal, he had been seeing another woman, Fiona Somebody, and had even been in her bed within the past twenty-four hours, was something she could not accept. It made her feel sick with anger at his duplicity, and her own naïveté.

I wonder he didn't invite her to the wedding. Oh, God, if I'd known this morning, I should have refused to go through with it, no matter how furious he was or how big a scandal it created, she thought with impotent fury.

Now what was to be done? Nothing. She was trapped. Or was she? Perhaps not.

She might be Drogo's wife in name now, but that didn't mean she was forced to submit her body to a repetition of the act which he had so recently performed with the witty, sexy Fiona.

For a few moments, such was her outrage that Annis actually toyed with the idea of slipping out of the building by a back way, leaving her bridegroom and all his guests to make what they chose of her dramatic disappearance.

Had she been in her going-away clothes, she might have carried out this enraged impulse, in spite of the other practical difficulties such as lack of funds and having nowhere to hide except in some cheap boarding-house where she might be recognised and given away, if not to Drogo then to the newspaper men who would be sure to follow up so sensational a turn of events.

But to leave the premises by stealth, and to hail a taxi while dressed in a bridal gown, and diamonds worth many thousands, was plainly an impossibility. She could walk out on Drogo, but not yet; not until they returned to the apartment where they would have two hours to rest before their flight to Paris.

Someone tapped on the door and a voice which she recognised as Diana's asked to come in.

Annis mustered all her powers of dissimulation and went to undo the bolt which fortunately made no sound as she drew it aside. When the older woman entered the room she was by the dressing-table putting on lipstick.

'Drogo's getting impatient. He sent me to hurry you up. I've seen him suddenly become bored at other sorts of receptions, but he can't walk out of this one without you,' said Diana, smiling.

'I'm just coming,' Annis replied.

She blotted her lips with a tissue and dropped it into the pink velvet-covered container on the floor at the side of the dressing-table. It surprised her that her hand was quite steady when, inwardly, she was shaking.

As she and Diana re-entered the crowded reception area,

her taut nerves flinched from the babel of sound and the atmosphere heavy with cigar smoke and many different scents. Not that the prospect of being alone with her bride-groom was any more welcome to her.

With the advantage of being a head or more taller than most of the people surrounding him, Drogo saw her before she had made her way through the press of guests, some of whom were beginning to draw aside to let her through.

She saw him coming to join her and remained where she was, wondering if any of the people staring at her could detect that her smile was a mask concealing all her real feelings which were a compound of humiliation and the first real hatred she had ever experienced.

She was conscious of a murmur spreading through the crowd, and of people craning to catch a final glimpse of the bride and groom before they departed.

To how many others, already, had the two unknown women passed on their titbit of scandal? As Drogo took hold of her arm, her instinct was to wrench free from the possessive grip of those fingers which only a short time ago had been caressing the woman known by half fashionable London to have been his mistress. To have been ... and to be still.

Is she jealous of me? Annis wondered. Or doesn't she care as long as he rewards her skill in bed in the customary way with extravagant presents?

Presently, for the third and last time that day, she stepped into the back of the huge black limousine, and Drogo made sure that her skirts and the folds of her veil would not be caught in the door before he took his place beside her.

As the car slid away from the kerb he said, 'I can't say I've ever much cared for wedding receptions, and my own has been no exception. You look a little pale, Annis. Did you do as I suggested and have a good breakfast this morning?'

'Yes ... some scrambled eggs. I'm not hungry.'

'I am—but not for food.' He reached for her hand and pressed it, his tawny eyes glittering with ardour as his gaze shifted to her mouth and then to the curves closely moulded by the tight-fitting bodice.

With a shudder of dismay she realised that, although she had been assuming that Paris would be the setting for her graduation from girlhood to womanhood, he might have it in mind to make love to her immediately they were alone.

She attempted to free her hand and, to her relief, he released it without apparently divining that her mood was now very different from the confident glow in which she had driven from the church to their wedding breakfast.

As on the two previous journeys, she noticed how women in the streets, if they spotted the beribboned car and the white-clad figure in the back, would automatically smile at her, as if the sight of a bride cheered them up and made them remember how it felt to be young and happy and about to set off on a honeymoon.

If only they knew, she thought dully.

For the rest of the way they were silent, which gave her time to think out a course of action if, on changing his grey morning coat and waistcoat, Drogo decided to have a shower.

She knew she could not rely on this happening. But, if it did, it would give her five or ten minutes to make her escape with the smaller of the two suitcases which contained all her worldly possessions, and which Theron had fetched from her digs and taken to Drogo's apartment before driving Mrs Leveson to the church.

How she could get away should Drogo not take a shower

she didn't know. But she meant to manage it somehow. There was no way in which he could make her accompany him to France, or force her to consummate a marriage in which her position, she now saw, was going to be very little better than that of a number one wife in a harem. And it was because she suspected that the powerful man sitting beside her was capable of exercising his rights by brute strength that she did not intend to explain her behaviour beforehand. He would learn why she had left him by letter.

Had she not been profoundly agitated, she would have wondered why, when the lift reached the top floor, the door of the apartment had not been opened by Theron when he heard the signal which sounded whenever someone pressed the lift button marked 7.

But even when Drogo used his key, it did not dawn on her that the apartment was empty.

As he stood aside to let her pass, she swept swiftly through the hall and into the sitting-room, her skirts and petticoats rustling on the thick carpet with a sound like a gust of wind disturbing a deep drift of leaves on an autumn morning.

Never having seen Drogo's bedroom, and not knowing where her suitcases would be, in the centre of the room she paused, her hands going up to her head to search for the diamond pins.

'Have those things made your head ache?' he asked, as he went to a table where a bottle of champagne was resting in a bucket of ice, and a number of covered silver dishes concealed, presumably, some sort of cold collation which either Drogo had ordered or Rosie might have prepared off her own bat.

In fact her hair-style had been perfectly comfortable, but

she answered, 'Yes, they have,' and placed them carefully on a side table, making a mental note not to forget to remove her engagement and wedding rings and leave them behind when she left.

'Some of this will soon put that right,' said Drogo, his accustomed hands releasing the cork from its cage and easing it gently out of the bottle while his gaze remained fixed on her face until the act of filling the two tall, slender-stemmed flutes made it necessary for him to look away.

'If you don't mind, I—I think I'll change before having anything to eat.' She tried to sound very casual.

'Why not? Much as that dress becomes you, it doesn't look particularly comfortable.'

'Are my other things in your room?'

'Our room now, Annis,' he corrected. 'Here you are, have a glass of this first to soothe the headache while you're undressing.'

'Thank you.' She took it from him, relieved when, without lingering beside her, he drank some wine and returned to the table to look underneath the covers.

'Let's see what Rosie has left for us. She warned me the bride and groom rarely have much to eat at the reception, however well the guests fare, and she was absolutely right.'

'Left for us . . . you mean she isn't here?'

'No, she and Theron and some of their relations are having a separate celebration at my expense. She and he would have been justifiably hurt not to be asked to the church, but they would have felt out of place afterwards. They'll enjoy themselves more on their home ground. You didn't want her to be here, did you?'

'No . . . no, not really,' said Annis lamely.

Drogo replaced the last of the lids. 'She did suggest com-

ing back to help you get out of your finery, but I told her
it wouldn't be necessary. I could cope with what you
couldn't manage.'

I'm sure you're an expert, was on the tip of her tongue.
But she bit back the acid retort and said, not entirely truth-
fully, 'Even the clients of couturiers don't always have
maids nowadays. I can manage myself, thank you.'

'Then I'll show you our room.'

It was at the end of a passage which, having no windows, was lit by a pool of light falling on the down-bent
carved stone head of some oriental deity. But the room to
which he led her was well lit by a wall-to-wall span of
large panes giving on to the end of the roof-garden with
daytime privacy provided by vertical sun-slats at present
in the open position, and night-time seclusion afforded by
curtains of aubergine linen. The same material was
stretched on the walls and formed a canopy over he bed.
The other colours were maroon and scarlet, and the effect
was both rich and masculine.

'This is part of a suite designed for the previous owner
by David Hicks,' Drogo told her. 'I liked this bedroom
and saw no reason to change it, but my predecessor's wife's
bedroom has been converted into a billiards room, leaving
only her bathroom and dressing-room for the use of my
future wife. If you find these colours too strong for you—
"vibrating" is the word which Hicks himself uses, I believe—you can ask him, or some other designer, to re-
decorate it to suit you.'

'It's very nice,' she said tonelessly.

'Your travelling clothes have been hung in here, in
the dressing-room,' he said, passing through a jib-door
made to look like part of the bedroom wall. 'Rosie has
packed all your trousseau things in one of my suitcases.

If there's anything you need to transfer from the cases brought over this morning, they should be here, too.' He opened the door of a cupboard. 'Yes, they are. She asked if you wanted her to unpack them completely while we're away, or if you would rather she left them until you come home. I told her I didn't know, and that you'd ring up from France and give her instructions yourself.'

'There are one or two things from the smaller case which I shall need,' said Annis, intending—when the opportunity arose—to snatch from the case the first street clothes which came to hand.

'I'll put the case on a rack for you.' He took from the side of the cupboard a folding luggage stand and, having set the case on it, unbuckled the straps. 'Where are your keys?'

'It must be in one of the other cupboards. Ah, yes, here we are.' He took the bag down from a high shelf above a rail from which was hanging the blonde wool crêpe suit and blouse in which Annis had been going to travel. 'But why not attend to that later? There's plenty of time. I think you should take off your dress, borrow one of my bathrobes, and just unwind for an hour.'

As he spoke, Drogo shrugged off his coat and, tossing it over his left arm, began to loosen the pewter silk tie he was wearing.

'I'm not wound up,' she said stiffly, as he urged her back to the bedroom, there to toss his coat over a chair.

'Aren't you, darling? I think you are. You've been visibly tense ever since we left the reception.' The tie went the way of his coat and, while his long fingers dealt with the buttons of his waistcoat, his other hand tipped up her chin. 'Smile for me, Annis—that lovely warm smile you gave me coming up the aisle. I'd never seen you looking so happy—or so beautiful,' he added.

If she hadn't discovered what manner of man he really was, she might have been grateful to be gentled out of her nervousness. As it was, only by an effort of will could she stop herself striking away his hand and telling him his touch had become repugnant to her.

'I was happy.'

Then, she added silently.

For an instant she thought he was going to kiss her, but instead he patted her cheek, and said, 'I'll fetch us both a robe.'

During his all too brief absence in his own dressing-room or bathroom, her hope of his taking a shower began to diminish. And how else could she escape?

He came back to find her biting her lips with vexation because she could not reach a fastening somewhere between her shoulderblades.

'That dress does need a maid. Let me help you,' he said, as he cast on the end of the bed two robes, one white and one navy.

Knowing that he was right, she could never extricate herself without his assistance, Annis let him deal with the tiny hooks and eyes which had defeated her.

'The dress having been undone, it comes off upwards, presumably?' he asked, a few seconds later.

'Yes, but I can manage that part of it.'

As Drogo opened the back, she clutched the dress to her in front, because the bodice was lined and needed no bra underneath it.

'But I should be delighted to help you,' he murmured, and she felt his breath warm on her spine before his lips brushed her skin. 'I should enjoy it . . . *ma femme*.'

'I would rather undress by myself ... please, Drogo!'

Recognising the unbridelike tone of her first answer, she tried, with the rider, to make it sound shy and appealing.

But, as she might have known, he was not the type of bridegroom to pander to maidenly modesty. Pushing the dress off her shoulders, he traversed her smooth naked back with a side-to-side sweep of light kisses which sent a long shudder through her as she thought that, a few hours ago, his warm lips had been softly nibbling another woman's sleek back.

No doubt Drogo thought it had been a shudder of excitement. Before she knew what he was doing, he had caught up the folds of her skirt and was lifting them over her head and, in so doing, enveloping her in a mass of silk which muffled her objections.

Had the dress been an off-the-peg garment, she would have resisted more strenuously. But the beauty of the silk and the perfection of the workmanship made her loath to risk any damage. She let him remove it, and then snatched up the front of the outermost petticoat and, holding it over her breasts, swung to face him with an expression which even the most obtuse bridegroom could not have misread.

His teasing expression became a look of astonishment. 'My dear girl, what *is* the matter?' he asked, his tone kind and concerned.

'*Everything* is the matter,' she said, with a break in her voice. 'I've made a terrible mistake. I—I can't endure being your wife.'

Drogo stared at her for a moment, then he took off his waistcoat and turned to toss it on the chair where he had already put his coat. Half turned away from her, he removed the links from his shirt cuffs and slipped them in his trousers pocket. Then he unbuttoned his shirt and pulled it free of the waistband of the pale grey trousers, their cavalry cut emphasising the length of his legs from his lean hips and flat, hard stomach down to the slight swell of his calf muscles.

'It's a little late to arrive at that conclusion, Annis,' he said calmly, as he shrugged the shirt off his broad brown shoulders. 'Our marriage is a *fait accompli*, and has been for several hours. Perhaps it's only just hit you that our lives are now bound together, and a spasm of panic isn't unnatural. I felt something of the sort myself, when I put the ring on your finger. But it didn't last more than a few seconds, and your nerves will calm down if you let them. There's nothing to be afraid of, I promise you.'

As he said this, he moved towards her, his hands outstretched as if to take her by the shoulders. But when she retreated, shrinking, he didn't follow but sat on the end of the bed to remove his socks and his shoes. Then, barefoot, he crossed to his dressing-room to reappear almost at once with his feet in black leather mules.

'I'm not afraid. You don't understand . . .' she began.

'If you aren't, you must be quite unusual. I should think most girls are, the first time. Now why not get rid of all those underpinnings and put something comfortable on, and then we'll go back to the sitting-room and finish the champagne.'

His tone of voice could not have been more reassuring. Indeed she had never heard him speak as gently before. But that kissing her had aroused him, and that his blood was still hot, became obvious when he took off his trousers and, clad only in light blue briefs of the briefest kind, reached for the white terry robe.

Watching him wrap it around himself and tie the sash to hold it in place, she realised that his relaxed, easy manner was like the places on a volcano where the crust of ground was so thin that one false step could release the fierce heat smouldering beneath it.

Striving to keep her voice steady, she said, 'You told me you were going to spend last night here, in the apartment, attending to business matters. But you didn't, did you? You went out?'

'Yes, I did. How did you know? Did you ring me up? Rosie didn't mention it to me. Why didn't you try again this morning? We could have talked, even if we weren't, by tradition, supposed to set eyes on each other.'

'I didn't find out by ringing you. I overheard some people talking at the reception. They ... they were expressing amazement that even a man of your sort should spend the night before his wedding in the arms of his ... his paramour.'

She had never seen Drogo enraged before, and it was alarming to watch the muscles knotting at his jaw, and his black brows drawn down over eyes which seemed all at once to have darkened and to be the eyes of a stranger who was glaring at her with such ferocity that it took all her courage to stand her ground.

'And how did these people come by this information? Were they under the bed?'

The questions were softly put, with his lips curling back from his teeth in a sneer which increased her fear of him.

'One of them saw you leaving her flat in the small hours and, not unnaturally, concluded that you'd been in bed with her.'

'And you, without hesitation, believed that it must be so?'

'What would you expect me to think? That the woman was making it up? That it couldn't possibly be true, because you're not the sort of man who would have a mistress? Perhaps you've forgotten, but I haven't, that the first time we met there was a girl in your party who was obviously there for your pleasure.'

'But that was a long time ago, and now I have you for my pleasure. Or so I hope—although if you continue to find excuses for keeping me at arm's length, I shall begin to think you're not only chaste but cold as well,' he said harshly.

'Excuses!' she flared, her eyes flashing. 'I'm not excusing myself, I'm accusing you. If what I heard isn't true, why don't you deny it? Although you've already admitted you did go somewhere last night.'

'I'll also admit that I went to the flat of a woman with whom, at one time, I did have a certain relationship. Being unmarried, why should I not? But it wasn't for that purpose that I went to see her last night.'

'For what purpose, then?' she demanded.

Drogo thrust his hands in the patch pockets of his robe, and the movement drew the cloth taut, outlining the power of his shoulders which were not only broad of bone but armoured with muscle. His ordinary clothes tended to conceal his strength, disguising rather than emphasising the fact that he was not merely a tall man but also a formidably tough one.

'For a reason which doesn't concern you,' he said, in a curt tone. 'If you're going to give credence to every piece of spiteful tittle-tattle, and be constantly jealous and suspicious of my relations with other women, you'll make yourself very unhappy and me very angry. The best way a woman can ensure that her husband is not unfaithful to her is by making him welcome in her bed. I've been patient long enough, Annis. I want you, and you're my wife. I won't be put off any longer.'

With which statement he moved towards her with a purposeful step which made her throat constrict with apprehension.

'You c-can't take me against my will,' she stammered hoarsely.

He gave her a mirthless smile. 'It won't be against your will,' he said, before he swept her into his arms.

It was useless to struggle. She knew that from the outset, but pride made her try to resist him, pounding her fists against his chest and twisting her face from side to side in a hopeless endeavour to avoid being kissed on the mouth.

For a short time he let her strike him and keep her lips out of reach. Then he made a sound deep in his throat which seemed to change from a chuckle at the futility of her resistance into a growl of impatience,

All at once her hands were behind her, pinioned by fingers like steel, while he held her face still for his kiss and she saw his strange tawny eyes burning lustfully down into hers.

But the hard, brutal kiss she expected did not happen. Drogo laid his mouth lightly on hers, and she felt the movements of his lips as he murmured, 'My pleasure is going to be your pleasure,' and began to kiss her until she could bear it no longer and, with a low groan of surrender, she unclenched her teeth and let her tense body relax.

Presently she felt his hand at her waist, searching for the fastening of the petticoat which had helped to give her wedding dress its beautiful line. It was actually three petticoats in one, with a layer of stiff tarlatan sandwiched between the outer and innermost layers of white silk taffeta with flounced hems bound with blue ribbon.

When Drogo discovered the clip which held the waist-band, the whole thing slid down her hips as gently as petals dropping from a white rose, and sank to the floor, leaving her naked but for her white silk stockings, the wisp of lace and satin ribbon which held them up, and the briefest of white crêpe-de-chine panties.

Her eyes shut, she felt him lift her and carry her to the bed. There he laid her down and she felt him take off her shoes before he sat down beside her, his warm fingers brushing her thighs as he undid the lacy suspenders and began to peel down her stockings.

Her forearms hiding her breasts, and her eyes tightly closed as if by shutting out the sight of it she could make her submission less shaming, Annis lay still, tension return-ing now that he was no longer pressing those intoxicating kisses on her mouth.

How expertly he does it, she thought bitterly as, with a palm under her calf, he lifted her leg to remove the stocking more easily. When both had been tossed aside, he undid the suspender belt and that, too, was swiftly dis-carded, leaving her in nothing but the flimsy *cache-sexe* hand-embroidered with a pale blue butterfly and with rouleaux bows on the hips.

Feeling sure her whole body was flushing, she expected to feel him unfastening the bows so that soon she would be naked as she had been the first time he saw her.

But instead she felt movements which indicated that he was removing his robe and perhaps his own briefs.

She trembled, her breathing rapid and shallow, her heart pounding under her wrist.

'Don't hide yourself from me.' As he spoke, he took her hands and unclasped them, drawing them upwards and outwards until they were resting on the pillows, still concealed by the bedspread. He held them there, loosely but firmly, while he bent down to rub his face against her smooth, creamy flesh and to murmur, 'How lovely they are ... like white peaches.'

The huskiness of his voice, and the slight roughness of his lean cheeks, sent a thrill of exquisite pleasure through her. But instead of yielding to it, a final flicker of rebellion made her make her voice sharp with hostility as she said, 'Lovelier than hers?'

She felt him recoil, and her eyes flew open to see him poised above her, looking furious again. It should have pleased her that her thrust had hit home, but somehow it didn't.

She wished she could retract the jibe, for at least his touch had been gentle, and if, now, she had made him decide to be ungentle with her ... she quailed at the thought.

For a moment longer Drogo loomed above her, and she understood then what it must have felt like to be a slave or a captive in the days when nearly all women had been at the mercy of men. Drogo let go her wrists and slid one strong arm underneath her, lifting her up in such a manner that her head was flung back, her long throat drawn like a bow for his warm mouth to trace and re-trace the smooth curve from chin to collarbone.

'It isn't enough to have an exciting young body,' he answered, close to her ear. 'You have to know how to use it, and you don't, do you?—— Not yet, my girl. But I have an idea you'll be an extremely apt pupil.'

And with lips and hands he began to complete his conquest of her.

*

When Annis woke out of a deep sleep, she seemed to be lying on her back beneath a gigantic mushroom. For some moments this illusion persisted until her mind cleared and the lines fanning out from a central point overhead came into focus. They were not after all the pale pink gills beneath the cap of a mushroom, but the radiated pleats of material lining the roof of Drogo's bed.

But Drogo was not in it with her. She was alone in the bed, and alone in the room.

It was no longer daylight. The aubergine curtains were drawn, and the bedroom was lit by one lamp with a dark red silk shade through which the bulb glowed like the embers of a dying fire.

Annis sat up and hitched the pillows into a comfortable mound behind her: four large pillows, filled with pure down judging by their softness, and cased in the finest percale. She had seen percale bedlinen in shops, but had never slept in it before. The sheets felt as different from ordinary cotton as real silk from synthetic imitations.

She wondered where Drogo had gone. Her last recollection, before emotional exhaustion had sent her to sleep, was that he had been lying beside her, propped up on one elbow, stroking back the tendrils of tumbled hair which had clung to her damp cheeks and forehead after that wild storm of feeling which had ended her girlhood and made her, at last, a woman.

For a while she sat pondering her first experience of the act which, although Mary Rossiter had explained it to her long ago, had, because of Annis's isolated upbringing and the kind of books she had read, retained a good deal of mystery for her.

Once, in the rest room at the store, unwittingly she had picked up a magazine containing pictures which had startled and repelled her; and sometimes she had been unable to avoid overhearing snatches of conversation between married women, and girls more worldly than she, which had made her realise that physical love was not always wonderful and uplifting. Now she knew for herself what it was like: or rather, she knew what it was like to lie in the arms of an expert lover who understood the female body better than she had herself.

But what she still didn't know—and never would—was what it was like to make love with one's heart and soul, not merely as an exercise in sensual pleasure.

The door opened and Drogo came in. He was fully dressed, and carrying a tray which he balanced on one hand while he closed the door behind him.

'Ah, you're awake,' he said, as he came to the bedside. He put the tray on the night table and switched on another less subdued lamp. 'I've made you a pot of tea—the traditional English restorative after an ordeal,' he added, his mouth quirking at one corner.

Then he sat on the bed and reached for her hand which he kissed, first on the back and then on the palm. 'But perhaps it wasn't quite the ordeal you expected, Mrs Wolfe.' There was a gleam in his eyes as he gave her her new name and title.

Suddenly Annis remembered that they had been supposed to be going to Paris this afternoon.

'Oh, the plane! Shall we miss it?' she explained. And, as she did so, she realised that she no longer intended to run away from him at the first opportunity. Their marriage was, as he had remarked earlier, a *fait accompli*—more so now than when he had said it.

Then, in spite of having been through a wedding ceremony, she had not felt inescapably bound to him. It was the surrender of her body which, for her, had set the seal on their marriage.

'That flight took off over an hour ago, but we didn't miss it because I rang up and cancelled it, and booked two seats on another flight tomorrow morning,' said Drogo.

He released her hand, reached for the tray and, letting down two supports concealed underneath it at either end, placed it across her lap.

'I thought, in the circumstances, it would be better for you to spend this evening resting. There's an old film on television which might amuse you, or we can listen to music.'

'Will you have to pay for the cancelled seats? And what about the hotel where we were going to stay tonight?' she asked.

'I've telephoned the hotel and told them to expect us tomorrow. Any slight extra expense involved——' He left the reply unfinished, his shrug dismissing the matter as unimportant.

Annis looked at the tray which, as well as the tea things, bore a small covered silver dish like the one owned by old Mrs Leveson, a relic of her prosperous past, which had a hot water compartment for keeping teacakes warm.

The dish on the tray, she discovered, contained slips of hot toast, cut thickly and glistening with butter. The sight of them made her realise how famished she was. The tea, although Drogo had joked about it, was precisely what she felt like drinking.

As she poured milk into the cup, it struck her that this moment of her life had many of the ingredients of great happiness. She was the wife of an enormously rich man who was also young and attractive and who, for the time being, was showing her great consideration.

But how could the physical comforts with which she was surrounded ever compensate for the pain of knowing that he was not in love with her, and that there was still another woman in his life?

'Shall I run a bath for you?' he suggested.

'Oh, thank you, but I can do it when I've finished this.'

'Let me do it for you. I have nothing else to do,' he answered.

The toast had cinnamon sprinkled on it, and it surprised her that he should be capable of going to the kitchen and finding everything necessary to prepare the tray for her. When he came back from her bathroom, she said this to him.

'I shouldn't rate myself as much of a man if I could only survive with people to wait on me. I only use the kitchen very occasionally, but it isn't an unknown territory to me,' he said. 'Have you finished?'

'Yes, thank you. It was delicious. If you wouldn't mind handing me that bath-robe, I'll get up now.'

Drogo removed the tray and set it aside. 'Do you find the temperature in here too cool for comfort?'

'No, it's beautifully warm.'

'Then why do you need a bath-robe?' As he spoke, he took hold of the bedclothes and tossed them aside, exposing her body down to the knees.

'*Oh!*' Annis couldn't repress the small sound of vexation and confusion.

That, before her sleep, there had been no part of her which he had not caressed had not made her immune to all further embarrassment.

'P-please, Drogo . . .' she protested, trying to recover the clothes.

As she reached forward to seize them, he took the soft

weight of one breast in the palm of his hand, making her recoil against the pillows, the colour in her flushed cheeks deepening.

'You'll have to learn not to be shy with me,' he said mockingly. 'It will be a long time before I tire of looking at you, my innocent Eve.'

But you will tire ... one day, she thought, and forced herself to sit still and endure his devouring gaze.

At last he stood up and strolled to the door, saying casually, over his shoulder, 'Take as long as you like in the bath.'

Annis took half an hour, from time to time letting out water and topping up from the hot tap. After having to share an old bath supplied by a tank which never provided enough hot water for a deep bath, it was luxury to have a bathroom exclusive to her, where the hot water was apparently inexhaustible and virtually boiling. Thick fleecy bath towels, warmed by a bank of heated towel rails, made climbing out a pleasure instead of an effort.

As the long sleep had calmed her mind, so the leisurely bath had soothed her physical discomfort. She supposed she had the unknown Fiona to thank for Drogo's patience with her. Surely there were very few bridegrooms who, after so restrained a courtship, would have been able to leash their ardour as he had?

Although in a way she was grateful that the pain of her initiation had been much less than she had expected, it was an ironic and displeasing thought that perhaps the first time would have been less agreeable if he had really loved her, and had not had his appetite dulled by Fiona's experienced embraces the night before.

It was only when, wrapped in a bath sheet, she returned to the bedroom that she realised that while she slept Drogo must have collected and put away all her wedding clothes.

She wondered what she should wear for the rest of the evening, and decided against a glamorous negligee which a normal bride would have chosen. Instead she put on a jade green cashmere sweater with a pleated skirt of the same colour.

Drogo was sitting in a high-backed leather wing chair, listening to a symphony, when she joined him. She would have sat down and kept silent until the music was over, but he sprang up as soon as he saw her.

'Time for some more champagne—and for more appropriate music,' he remarked.

Moments later the symphony stopped and soon she recognised Stephen Sondheim's *Do I Hear A Waltz*?

He was one of her favourite modern songwriters, whom she had discovered through working in the cosmetics department where music was played to put customers in a spending mood. But she wouldn't have expected Sondheim's romantic music to have a place in Drogo's record collection.

He brought her the champagne and, when she had taken it, put his arm lightly round her and began dancing on the spot as if, instead of being in his spacious living-room, they were surrounded by people in some dimly lit night-club.

For something to say, Annis said, 'Rosie and Theron will be surprised to find us here when they come back.'

'Yes, and as we shall have gone to bed before them, I'd better have a word with Brown, the night porter, and ask him to warn them that we're still here.'

Bed. Would she ever be able to hear him say that word without feeling a vibration of the nerves? Annis wondered. Would he want to possess her again? She had no idea how often people made love. 'My innocent Eve' he had called her, and she knew that she was, and regretted it. It meant that she had no weapons to defend herself against him, and against that other woman who was so amusing and sexy that, had he not wanted children, Drogo would not have taken a wife.

For a little while, watching the film on television, Annis was absorbed and relaxed, forgetting the tall, long-legged man lounging on the sofa beside her, all her attention on the screen.

But then came the ten o'clock news and, after reports of world events, she was startled by a shot of herself stepping out of the car at the church, followed by a picture of them both.

How happy I looked, she thought, amazed. But of course I didn't know then that I was going to have to share him with her, with Fiona.

The bulletin ended and Drogo switched off the set. They finished the food which Rosie had left for them, supplemented by more good things which he had found in the refrigerator.

'A long day calls for an early night, don't you think?' he said, when they had finished.

'Yes ... if you like,' she said hollowly.

'I like.' His expression was quizzical, as if he guessed her uncertainty and derived a sadistic amusement from it.

They went to the bedroom together, but there they parted to go to their separate bathrooms. Annis spent as long as she dared taking off her make-up and brushing out her long hair. Then she put on a filmy nightdress of virginal white chiffon—only one of several in her trousseau—and the double-chiffon peignoir which went with it.

Drogo was pacing the room in the navy blue robe when she rejoined him. She closed the door of her dressing-room and stayed by it, nervously watching him.

He came to her and took her hand which he laid against his hard jaw. 'Was my chin rough earlier on? I shall have to shave twice a day if I'm not to spoil your soft skin.'

'I—I didn't notice any roughness.'

'You were too frightened of me,' he said. 'You aren't frightened now, are you, Annis?'

She didn't answer. It wasn't fear of him she felt, but something more complex, something she couldn't explain, even to herself.

'Love can never be very enjoyable for a woman at first. But it gets better—that I can promise you,' he said quietly.

But it isn't love, merely sex, she wanted to fling at him. *You don't love me. You never will. I'm only the girl you've chosen to give you your children.*

She would have withdrawn her hand, but he caught it between both of his.

'You don't still think, do you, that our marriage is a mistake, and that you can't stand being my wife?' His gaze was piercingly intent. It seemed to bore into the innermost places of her mind.

She avoided his eyes. 'Perhaps not. I'm not sure yet, Drogo.'

With a change of mood so abrupt that it made her gasp, he snatched her into his arms and pressed a long, sensuous kiss on her parted lips.

'I'll make you sure. I'll make you want me ... and love me,' he told her harshly.

She felt his voice had the ring, not of a man making a vow to his wife, but of someone determined to break in a wild, nervous filly.

A shudder went through her. Drogo felt it, and reacted by swinging her up in his arms and carrying her to the bed. Earlier, after her bath, she had made it tidy and put the cover in place. Since then he had turned it down. For a moment she thought he was going to fling her upon it and take her for his own enjoyment, not caring if she was responsive. Perhaps, for a second or two, that was his intention. But then, after setting her down, he loosened the tie of her peignoir before switching off the light on that side of the bed and walking to the far side.

As she slipped the garment off her shoulders and laid its diaphanous folds across the foot of the bed, she saw him also disrobing, and involuntarily her gaze lingered on his impressive physique, his brown skin gilded by the lamplight.

He was tanned everywhere except for a very small area around the loins, and even that was not white. With his dense black hair and tawny eyes, he had also inherited the olive skin of the Greeks.

'As you used to sunbathe, so I sleep,' he said, seeing her covert gaze on him.

There seemed no answer to this. Annis stepped out of her white velvet mules and climbed into bed and lay down, her whole body quivering with renewed nervous tension.

Drogo took one of the two pillows on his side and tossed it on to a chair before he turned out the lamp and climbed in beside her. The bed was so wide that, in doing so, he didn't brush against her as he might have done in an ordinary bed.

He lay down, and stretched, and lay still. She thought, with relief, that in spite of that long hungry kiss he might be going straight to sleep. She longed for her own single bed where she could have let her tears flow instead of holding them back so that her throat ached and her tightly closed eyelids smarted. For the first time in her life she was sharing a room, and yet she had never felt more lonely than with this alien male presence beside her in the darkness.

When he moved, and his hand touched her waist, her self-control almost snapped. But she managed to choke back the plea to be left to herself.

She could not tell when it was that his light caresses stopped being a test of her endurance and became a repetition of the voluptuous sensations he had made her experience earlier.

He leaned over her, kissing her eyelids. But when a sigh parted her lips, and she would not have minded receiving a more ardent kiss, his mouth would come close to hers and then move away. And when she was languorous with pleasure, her tears and forlornness forgotten because of the blissful feelings he had once again induced in her, Drogo did not slake his own appetite, but said, 'Go to sleep now. Goodnight.'

Lapped in the afterglow of his love-play, and too drowsy to puzzle for long over its unexpected conclusion, Annis did as he bade her, and slept.

She was woken next morning by the chink of metal on glass. She opened her eyes to find Rosie lightly tapping a teaspoon against the rim of a beaker of orange juice on the breakfast tray she had placed on the night table.

'Good morning, madam,' she said, beaming. 'I'm sorry to wake you, but Mr Wolfe left orders that you were to be called not a minute later than ten o'clock. You have to leave for the airport at eleven, and he didn't want you to be rushed.'

'Good morning,' said Annis, sitting up. 'You say Mr Wolfe *left* orders. Where is he? Has he gone out?'

'Not for long. He''s just popped round to Harvey & Gore. Oh, dear, maybe I shouldn't have told you.'

'Why not? Who are Harvey & Gore?'

Rosie hesitated. 'They're jewellers, madam. Mr Wolfe always buys his birthday and Christmas presents for his aunts there. They specialise in antique jewellery which Mrs Ford and Miss Wolfe prefer to the new kind. I shouldn't wonder if Mr Wolfe has gone there to see if they've something nice you would like. So I ought not to have spoiled the surprise by letting on where he was going.'

'It doesn't matter, Rosie. I shan't let him know that you did. Goodness, what a huge breakfast!'—this after peeping under the cover on a plate on which were arranged several crispy grilled rashers of bacon with kidneys, mushrooms, a fried tomato and some cress.

'It's what Mr Wolfe had this morning, and he said you would have the same. I did tell him that usually ladies didn't like the substantial breakfast which most gentlemen enjoy, but he said that you didn't need to diet.'

'I haven't so far, but I should think I might if you fed me like this every morning. No, I'd like to brush my teeth first, please'—as the housekeeper would have transferred the tray to the bed.

When Annis came back from the bathroom, Rosie had plumped up the pillows and was waiting to lift the tray into place for her.

'There are two lovely photographs of you in *The Times* and the *Telegraph*, madam,' she said, indicating the folded newspapers tucked into a pocket at the end of the tray. 'And there's an even better one in our paper, but I didn't bring that in to you because Mr Wolfe might see it and be annoyed.'

'Why should he be that?' asked Annis.

'He doesn't approve of our paper, says it's a terrible rag. Well, I suppose he's right really, but it suits me. I couldn't plough through all that serious stuff he reads. I like news about the television stars and—but I mustn't hang about chatting or your breakfast will be getting cold. I'll come back and run your bath in about fifteen minutes, shall I?'

'Thank you, that would be fine.' Annis wondered how long it would take her to accustom herself to being waited on.

At the door, Rosie turned. 'There's just one thing I would like to say, if you won't take it wrong, madam?'

'I'm sure I shan't. What is it, Rosie?'

'I'm ever so pleased that you've come here. Theron and me, we couldn't wish for a better employer than Mr Wolfe. Providing people come up to scratch, there's never a cross word from him. But I've always looked forward to having a lady of the house—if she was a nice one, that is.'

'I should have thought you would feel just the reverse. An extra person in the household must make more work for you,' said Annis.

'Yes, perhaps, but it's work I enjoy. I love looking after beautiful clothes, and cooking for someone who'll notice every little detail, the way gentlemen don't, even the best of them.'

Annis smiled. 'Thank you very much, Rosie. It's reassuring to know that you don't resent my arrival.'

'Oh, no, Mrs Wolfe, not a bit. I thought you were ever so sweet the first time you came here to dinner. I hoped you might be the one who Mr Wolfe would lose his heart to—and I was right, wasn't I?'

Rosie whisked herself out of the room, leaving Annis to

regret that the housekeeper's view of their marriage was not a more accurate one.

She was having her bath when Drogo returned. She had neglected to lock the door, and when he tapped and called to her, 'May I come in?' she had no choice but to say 'Yes.'

When first she had stepped in the bath, the surface had bubbled with Dior's foamy *Bain Moussant*, lavishly tipped in by Rosie. Now the delicate bubbles had evaporated, leaving only the sea-blue colouring.

She had been lying at full length, but as Drogo opened the door she sat up and drew up her knees so that less of her would be exposed to view. He had said she must learn not to be shy of him, but on this, the first full day of her married life, her shyness was still intense.

'Did you mind that I wasn't there to kiss you good morning when you woke up?' Drogo asked.

Before she could answer, he sat on the edge of the bath and, resting a hand on the inner edge to keep his balance, bent down to kiss her on the mouth.

'I needed to stretch my legs,' he said, as he straightened.

'Rosie said you'd gone for a walk,' Annis told him. 'She's a dear little person. I thought she might be slightly hostile, but when she brought me my breakfast she made a little speech of welcome.'

'She would be foolish to be anything but welcoming,' he said dryly. He glanced at his watch. 'How long does it take you to make up your face?'

'Oh ... five or ten minutes. Not long.'

He rose and reached for one of the apricot bath sheets which he held for her, much in the manner that he might have held a long evening cloak.

'Out you come, mermaid,' he said, and she saw by the glint in his eyes that he knew she had been hiding herself from him, and was forcing her to stand up in front of him because it amused him to make her blush vividly.

By herself, she would have dried while standing in the bath with the water running out in order not to make the bath mat soggy. But with Drogo's teasing eyes on her, she stepped out in one hurried movement, and the several mirrors reflected her glistening nudity and the rosiness of her face under the pile of pale hair which she had pinned up anyhow, to be brushed and arranged properly later.

As he wrapped the towel round her, he laughed and, pulling her into his arms, gave her a vigorous hug.

'I think I shall be rather sorry when I can no longer make you blush,' he said, speaking over her head. When she was barefoot his tall figure towered over hers. His voice thickened as he added, 'But perhaps there'll be compensations.'

As his mouth touched one damp bare shoulder not enveloped by the towel, Annis felt his surge of desire and knew that, had there been more time, he would have made love to her.

Instead of which he released her and went swiftly out of the bathroom. When she returned to the bedroom she found she had it to herself.

She had forgotten about Harvey & Gore by the time she joined Drogo in the living-room where he was reading the financial pages of *The Times*.

He let the paper fall and rose. 'I bought this for you on my walk. It seemed to go with that green thing you wore last night.'

Something made of jade? Annis wondered, before she saw, by the wrapping, that his present could not be a jewel.

Nor was it from Harvey & Gore, but from Céline in Bond

Street, an expensive shop selling clothes of the utmost elegance and superb French accessories.

The gift was a pure silk scarf with a cream ground and a design inspired by peacocks' tail feathers, the colours including the shade of her cashmere sweater.

It was very much to her taste and, had Rosie not mentioned the jewellers, she would have received it with pleasure, surprised and warmed by his attention to her clothes.

But even as she said, 'Thank you. It's charming,' she had the chilling conviction that the scarf was a sop to Drogo's conscience because, before buying it, he had chosen a more lavish gift for the other woman in his life.

The thought lay like a canker at the back of her mind all that day, spoiling her enjoyment of the flight and of their arrival in Paris where Miss Howard had booked a suite at the *grande luxe* Plaza-Athénée on the Avenue Montaigne.

Annis had heard of the two famous Paris restaurants, Maxim's and the Tour d'Argent, but that night they dined at Lasserre, less widely known to foreigners but equally highly rated by French gourmets and those who knew Paris well.

They both had the *sole normande,* the poached fillets of fish being surrounded by oysters and mussels, with a rich sauce combining the flavours of wine, cream, butter and shellfish, and a garnish of mushrooms.

They did not talk much while they ate, the food deserving and receiving most of their attention. But later, over coffee and armagnac liqueur brandy, Drogo talked to her about France, explaining how, while the English industrial revolution had taken place in the previous century, the basis of France's economy had not changed from agriculture to industry until after the second world war;

and the French had now, in his opinion, overtaken British progress.

Later, in the taxi which took them back to their hotel, he said, 'You have the ability, very rare among women, of giving your whole mind to the matter in hand—whether it's something good to eat, or my exposition of French economics. It isn't a subject which interests you greatly, I imagine, but I never saw your attention wandering. I liked that.'

Against her will his praise warmed her. Since leaving the restaurant she had begun to feel on edge again. Obviously he would make love to her, and if, in the manner of a Victorian wife, she could have suffered it unmoved, she would have felt less degraded. But she knew she would not be unmoved, and it made her feel sick and ashamed that her dread of the hours ahead was tinged with excitement.

Going up to their suite in the lift, Drogo said, 'Did you bring any walking shoes?'

'I have one pair of low heels—yes.'

'Are you up to a walk, or are you tired?'

'A walk would be fine.'

So they went for the first of their several long night walks in Paris, and he showed her the Faubourg St Honoré with its tempting shop windows, and the mansion which had once belonged to Napoleon's sister and was now the British Embassy in which Berlioz and Thackeray had married, and Somerset Maugham had been born.

It was almost midnight before they returned to their suite.

'Are you going to have a bath?' Drogo asked.

'Yes, I think I will.' Anything to postpone going to bed with him.

There was a telephone in the bathroom. Annis was

soaping her shoulders when it emitted a sound which, some moments later, she recognised as the noise made by some extension sets when the main was brought into use. Drogo must be making a call.

At first she assumed that he was ordering something from Room Service. But when minutes elapsed with no second tinkle to signal the replacement of the receiver, a thought occurred which, in spite of the warmth of the bathroom and the hot water up to her waist, made her shiver with cold. Was he calling someone in London? Had he suggested a bath to her in order to have time to speak to his 'close friend' Fiona?

She could have verified her suspicion merely by picking up the extension receiver. But that was against her code. One did not, in any circumstances, listen in to other people's telephone calls. To interrupt them was another matter.

In a sudden frenzy of haste she leapt out of the bath and, without bothering to dry herself, shrugged on a long sea-green robe of velvety cotton. It had mules to match and she thrust her slim feet inside them and crossed the bedroom to the door of the sitting-room.

It was not quite shut. The well-oiled hinges made no sound as she pushed it open and saw her husband looking out at the lights of the city, with the telephone held to his ear.

She heard him say, 'I'll try to call you again tomorrow, but it may not be possible. Goodnight, Fiona.'

And in that instant, swept by anger and jealousy, she knew that Drogo had no need to make her love him. She already did, and perhaps had done so all along.

He put down the receiver and continued to stand with his back to her, unaware of her presence, thinking her still in the bathroom. Silently she retreated.

CHAPTER FIVE

ANNIS locked herself in the bathroom and thought about what she should do. Drogo's behaviour was damnable, utterly despicable. But she had already confronted him with it once, only to be told that jealousy would get her nowhere, and her best recourse was to make him so welcome in her bed that he did not need anyone else.

To confront him again would be useless: it would only serve to make him furious, and to upset her even more. How could she have failed to realise until tonight that when she felt for this man went much, much deeper than mere attraction?

No wonder she had been convinced there was no danger that she might fall in love with someone else after her marriage to him. She had been in love then—with him—but somehow she had not recognised her condition for what it was.

It was only tonight, after listening to him in the restaurant, and then walking about the city with him and realising how life-enhancing it was to have a husband who spoke the language of the country and could tell her interesting things about the theatres and the buildings, only then had it started to dawn on her that Drogo's mind had a power over her as strong as his physical magnetism.

There was a tap at the door which, totally absorbed by this self-revelation, she did not answer. He tried the handle and, finding the door locked, called, 'Annis, are you all right?'

'Yes ... yes. I shan't be much longer.' Swiftly she bent to dabble her hand in the water to make it sound as if she were still in the bath.

'There's no hurry.' He went away, and she heard a French newsreader's voice which might be coming from the radio in the bedroom or the television in the sitting-room.

She pulled the plug out of the outlet and, while the bath emptied, began to brush her teeth which, thanks to her mother's insistence on regular checks and a childhood without any sweets, had never been filled or extracted.

She had already creamed off her make-up and, after she had unpinned and brushed her hair, there was nothing to keep her in the bathroom but an overwhelming reluctance to face her husband until she had come to terms with the shattering insight which had come to her when she heard him say *Goodnight, Fiona.*

Above all, she felt she could not endure his lovemaking. Yet how was she to escape it? Plead a headache? Claim that her throat was sore and she thought she must be starting a cold? Somehow she could not see Drogo accepting either of those excuses as an adequate reason for forgoing his conjugal rights on the second night of their marriage.

The only way to keep him at arm's length was to tell him she had overheard the last part of his telephone call, and there was no way she would sleep with him while he kept up another relationship. But to say that would lead to a row which, as she had already decided, could only worsen the situation.

Suddenly, while she was wishing that some major crisis in the business world would demand Drogo's instant return to London, and give her the respite she needed in which to work out whether a one-sided love match was more or

less endurable than a marriage without love, she found
that nature had already come to her rescue.

Diana had warned her that the excitement and strain of
wedding preparations sometimes had this effect. In the
circumstances it was not a disaster but a reprieve.

Drogo was drinking champagne and watching a chat show
when she went to the sitting-room. Knowing that she could
not follow more than an occasional word of the fast, idio-
matic French, he at once switched off. Rather awkwardly,
but without mincing matters, she explained what had happened.

She had thought Drogo might show irritation, but he
couldn't have been nicer or more understanding, and that
in itself raised his stock with the part of her which wanted
him to be perfect, or as nearly perfect as anyone could
reasonably expect another human being to be.

She had been in bed for nearly an hour before he joined
her. Had she been asleep, his quiet movements would not
have disturbed her.

He seemed to go to sleep immediately, but she remained
wakeful a long time, her mind in a whirl of confused and
conflicting thoughts about him and herself and their future
together.

Afterwards, Annis wondered if there could ever have been
a stranger honeymoon. And yet, for all its dark undercurrents, it had not been wholly unhappy; on the surface, not
unhappy at all.

They had lunched or dined at all the best restaurants—
Le Grand Véfour, Les Belles Gourmandes, Taillevant,
Chez Albert and others—and sampled the cream of French
cuisine.

They had seen works of art which she would remember

for ever; Rodin's sculpture *The Kiss* and, at the Musée Marmottan, a large collection of paintings by Monet including the one called *Impression—Sunrise* which had given the press of the day their nickname for the group of artists whose first exhibition in 1874 had been mocked by the critics but which, now, would be worth millions.

Another day Drogo ordered a car to take them to the suburbs of Paris to see the Château de Malmaison where Napoleon had lived with the beauty from Martinique before he became Emperor and Josephine, lonely and bored, had run up colossal debts.

As if he felt Annis might grow weary of too much history and art, in between these cultural expeditions Drogo insisted on escorting her to see the collections of several *couture* houses.

At Yves St Laurent—in spite of her protests that she already had more than enough clothes—he insisted on her ordering an evening dress. When she had seen it modelled, it had not particularly appealed to her. But when she had the first fitting, which was arranged with all speed as her husband was already known at the house, and seemed to be regarded as a potentially important customer, it became apparent that he understood what suited her better than she did.

By the time they returned to London she had grown accustomed to spending her days and nights with him. As far as she knew he had made no more calls to Fiona. When their aircraft landed at Heathrow she had long since decided that, if he tried to find an excuse to visit his mistress later that day, she would do her best to frustrate the intention.

Beyond kissing her cheek every morning and again at bedtime, and holding her hand when she stepped out of taxis and hired cars, Drogo had not touched her. He appeared to be waiting for some kind of signal from her, and his manner showed no impatience.

In the car, driven by Theron, which took them back to his apartment, he said to her, 'I have tickets for the play at the Lyric Theatre tonight, but I think we'll let Rosie feed us as there aren't any restaurants in London to compare with the best in Paris.'

Concluding from this that he did not intend to desert her, Annis began to act on her plan for the future. She slipped her hand into his and said shyly, 'Paris was wonderful for me. I ... I'm sorry that, in some ways, it was disappointing for you.'

He looked at her thoughtfully for a moment, before lifting her hand to his lips and pressing a kiss on her knuckles. 'We have many years ahead of us,' was his reply.

Then he replaced her hand on her lap and turned to look out of the window. Annis wondered where his thoughts lay, and if there was any real hope that her plan could succeed.

Although they had been away for less than a week, there was a large pile of mail awaiting his return. Much of it he discarded after a cursory glance, explaining that he had long been, and from now on she too could expect to be, bombarded with dubious begging letters and the wild outpouring of cranks.

'These will be your province from now on,' he went on, tossing two or three cards of invitation on to her lap. 'Tomorrow you'd better go to Smythsons and buy a hostess book. From now on I shall rely on you to manage our social life and to keep track of the chops we owe.' Seeing that this expresion was unfamiliar to her, he added explanatorily, 'The invitations we've accepted and, sooner or later, must return. You'll have to consult me at first about which to accept or refuse, but you'll soon get to know the ropes.'

The curtain went up at the Lyric Theatre at eight o'clock, and they were to dine in two stages, having soup and a light main course beforehand, and the pudding and cheese when they came home.

Drogo often did this, Rosie told Annis. It avoided dining too early and hurriedly beforehand, or indigestibly late afterwards.

'Not that Mr Wolfe has ever had any trouble with his digestion. But a lot of his friends have trouble with ulcers and suchlike, and have to be careful what they eat. Although I shall never believe that it's fresh cream and country butter which bring on ulcers and heart attacks,' she declared in an adamant tone.

She was unpacking Annis's clothes, while Annis herself was arranging her cosmetics in the drawers of a dressing-table which had been installed in her absence.

'How can good food hurt anyone? It's the stuff they spray on the crops now, and the pills they give calves and chickens, which do the harm, if you ask me.'

Rosie continued to chatter on what was clearly a pet subject until Drogo came into the bedroom, at which point she discreetly disappeared.

'You mustn't let Rosie become a nuisance. Given the slightest encouragement, she'll talk the hind leg off a donkey,' he said when they were alone.

Annis laughed. 'Thank you for this,' she said, tapping the top of the dressing-table. 'You think of everything.'

'It was Rosie's thought, not mine. I just told Miss Howard to ring up Hicks' shop in Jermyn Street and ask them to organise something which would go with the rest of the room. If it isn't quite what you want, have them change it,' Drogo answered offhandedly.

She had meant to follow her thanks by getting up from the bench which went with the dressing-table and crossing the room to give him a kiss on the cheek, a mute sign that she was ready to re-establish their marriage on the new terms which she had thought out in the past few days.

However, his discouraging disclaimer about the dressing-table made her decide to wait until after the theatre before attempting the first tentative advance she had ever made to him.

Previously, her rôle had been one of passive submission or nervous retreat. But from now on, she saw, she would have to become more forthcoming; never to the extent of telling him what lay in her heart, but at least by inviting his lovemaking instead of merely submitting to it.

To go to the theatre she changed into a very feminine dress of fine black lace; the kind which Diana said had never gone out of fashion for more than a season or two since she was a girl, and one which had all the features which appealed to male eyes, even if they didn't turn other women's heads.

In fact as soon as he saw it, Drogo remarked, 'I like that,' and his gaze took in the close-fitting waist and the skirt which clung to her hips before flaring into a full swirling hemline. Although the dress was modestly high-necked, with a double ruff under her chin and double frills at the wrists of the long sleeves, it did not escape his notice that under the flower-patterned meshes of the lace, the silk underslip was a good deal less decorous. Several times during the first part of their dinner Annis caught his glance on her pale skin where the lace seemed to give it a pearly lustre, and the gleam in his eyes made her heart beat faster.

The play was a sophisticated comedy which she was

enjoying until a laughing glance at her husband showed his dark face set in the lines of complete abstraction. Where was he, while all about him people roared at the joke which had made her turn to exchange a glance with him? Even as she looked at him, he shook off his thoughts and became infected by the amusement reverberating round the auditorium, even though he had not heard the line which had caused it.

But the look she had seen on his face made her wonder uneasily if he would have preferred to spend the evening *à deux* with Fiona. Who was she? Where did she live? How long had she been Drogo's 'friend'? Did Diana know about her, and was that why Mrs Baird had seemed uncertain about the wisdom of their marriage?

'Are you not feeling well? Do you want me to take you home?'

It was Drogo's turn to catch Annis at a moment of inattention from the play.

'Oh, no—no, I'm fine,' she whispered back.

Afterwards they went home on foot. It was a fine night, and the heels of her black patent sandals were not so high as to make the short walk uncomfortable for her.

Catching shadowy glimpses of their reflection in the shop windows which were not alight, she seemed to see a stranger passing by. Could that woman wrapped in furs, with real diamonds in her ears, be herself?

Another couple came towards them and, as they drew abreast, Annis saw interest and perhaps a faint tinge of envy in the girl's eyes as she noticed the sable jacket over the cobwebby lace blowing back against Annis's legs as a sudden breeze caught it. But although the girl was wearing a shabby anorak, she and her young man had their arms entwined, their bare fingers interlocked, and they emanated an air of being completely happy in each other's company, even if they did not and perhaps never would have many material assets.

As they passed out of sight, Annis was sharply conscious that she and Drogo were walking like people on formal terms, not like newlyweds, not like lovers.

I will make him love me. I must! she thought, with fierce resolution.

Back at the apartment, they concluded the meal begun earlier, and then Annis said, 'I—I think I will go to bed now. I wonder if you'd mind helping me with my dress, Drogo? It has several tiny hooks and eyes which are impossible to manage alone. I had to ask Rosie to fasten them for me.'

'By all means.'

It was not very late but, before following her to the bedroom, he switched off the lights in the sitting-room, making it clear that he did not mean to return there to read or watch television as he had every night while in Paris.

In the bedroom she bent to unfasten the buckles of her sandals and slip them off her feet. Then she glanced over her shoulder at her husband, who was still standing inside the door with one of his more inscrutable expressions.

'Could you undo me now, please?' Her voice was not perfectly steady.

What was about to happen was no longer the unknown experience it had been the last time she had stood in this room and needed his help with the fastenings of her wedding dress. Nor did she expect, this time, to feel anything but pleasure in his arms. It was shyness, not apprehension, which made her tremble as he crossed the space between them.

It took him very little time to locate the hooks and eyes

and then to draw down the fastener which went from the nape of her neck almost to her spine.

'Why were you looking unhappy at one stage of the play tonight?' he asked her. As he spoke, she felt him run one finger very slowly down her bared back.

'I—I suppose for a moment my mind had gone off on some tangent or other. I can't remember what I was thinking,' she answered untruthfully. She turned, lifting her face to his. 'K-kiss me, Drogo.'

His arms closed round her, crushing her to his strong frame. She saw in his eyes the fierce, lion-like gleam of desire from which she had shrunk on their wedding day.

But now she had had several days in which to steel herself to accept the cruel disillusionment which had knocked her sideways at the reception; and now, too, she knew that she loved him—and loving was giving, not taking. Giving him all that he asked of her ... her body, and the children she would bear for him.

She slid her arms up round his neck, closed her eyes and parted her lips and, in doing so, felt a convulsive shudder run through him.

Drogo's first long, deep, scorching kiss made it clear that his patience in Paris had been but a thin veneer containing a need as powerful and irresistible as a vortex. Once swept into that swirling current of violent emotion, she could not have freed herself had she tried.

But she did not try: she surrendered herself to him utterly, yielding her mouth to kiss after kiss, each one more demanding than the last, and her body to his roving hands.

'How delicious you smell,' he said thickly, his lips on her neck.

Then he pulled the combs out of her hair, and the long

silky tresses fell out of the elegant coils in which she had arranged them for the theatre, and cascaded over his hands while he took off her dress and left her in nothing but a transparent strapless bra, French panties of oyster charmeuse and the sheerest of sheer black stockings held up by black garters.

'Turn off the light, Drogo ... please,' she whispered, when he had carried her to the bed and was looking with hot, hungry eyes at her pale thighs and heaving breasts while, with impatient brown fingers, he wrenched off his tie and swiftly removed his own clothes.

'No, no, I want to look as well as touch. You please my eyes as well as my hands,' was his answer.

'Not yet ... not tonight ... *please*, Drogo!'

Her voice and her eyes appealed to him to indulge her in this one repression until she was able to shed her last trace of shyness.

'All right ... not tonight, my lovely,' he agreed, with the ghost of a laugh.

He bent to switch off the lamp, her last sight of him being broad bronzed shoulders, and the hard-muscled planes of his chest.

Then the room was plunged into darkness in which, as he gathered her close to him, she found it easier to accept his expert mastery of her.

The next day, their honeymoon over, Drogo went to his office, leaving Annis to spend as she chose the hours until his return.

He had already gone when she woke. He had told her it was not unusual for him to be at his desk two hours before everyone else. Nevertheless it was a surprise to find him not there when she opened her eyes on that first morning back in London.

A surprise, and something of a relief because when she remembered those rapturous moments in the dark her face burned with swift hot colour.

As before she had breakfast in bed, although she told Rosie firmly that she did not intend to make a habit of it.

Later, when she was dressed, the housekeeper showed her the kitchen and the staff quarters. After which, as Drogo had suggested, she put on a coat and walked to Bond Street and the fashionable stationers where he had an account to which she could charge a large volume, bound in red leather, in which to record the details of their entertaining.

Passing the shop, further along, where Drogo had bought her the peacock's feather silk scarf reminded her of the woman who, somewhere in London, might be preparing to welcome him back into her life.

How should I ever know if he were to spend an hour or two with her this afternoon? Annis thought helplessly. Nothing could be more easy than for him to lead a discreet double life. Miss Howard would never betray him.

She walked on, quickening her pace, pushing these troublesome thoughts to the back of her mind.

However, when Drogo came home half an hour before she expected him and, finding her in the bedroom where she had just put on a housegown of plum red georgette, kissed her lips and held her against him, it was not the behaviour of a man coming home to his wife fresh from the arms of his mistress.

'Are you going to s-swim?' she asked breathlessly, thrown into confusion by that possessive kiss.

'If you have no better suggestion.' He began to loosen his tie, not as hurriedly as the night before, but with the same light in his eyes as they dwelt on the contours revealed by the thin, clinging house-gown.

The sight of his strong brown neck, now exposed by his

unbuttoned collar, always made a pulse beat in her own throat. But she knew she wasn't yet ready to make love in daylight.

'I—I thought you always had a swim,' she said.

'I usually did—in my bachelor days. But now I have a wife to consider. Have you missed me today?'

She wasn't sure how to answer him. By nature truthful and open, she found any form of deception an uneasy rôle for her. Had Drogo loved her, she would have missed him and counted the hours to his return. But because he was not in love with her, and she must keep hidden her own love, the day had seemed short rather than long.

'You didn't miss me,' he said dryly, and turned away towards his dressing-room.

Now I've annoyed him, she thought. I should have said, 'Yes, of course'. How very unreasonable men are! I don't suppose that I've even crossed his mind, but it irks his male amour propre that I haven't been pining for him.

'Shall I have a swim with you?' she suggested, when he reappeared.

'If you wish, by all means. But have you a bathing cap? If not, your hair will get wet, and it takes some time to dry, I imagine.'

'Yes—yes, it does,' she agreed. 'I'll buy myself a cap tomorrow.'

He said, 'That reminds me: I've been in touch with my bank about an account for you. Naturally all my resources are now at your disposal. But I think it may be less complicated if, rather than having a joint account for our personal spending, you have one of your own, and a quarterly allowance which can be increased if you find it less than you need. The bank will require your signature. I told them you'd go in within the next day or two.'

'Thank you, Drogo.'

'You don't have to thank me. It's the duty of a husband to support his wife.'

There was a clipped note in his voice, and a faint emphasis on the word 'duty' which made Annis wonder if he was angry because, a few minutes before, he had sensed her extreme reluctance to fulfil her duty to him.

She wanted to run to him, to cling. To say to him, 'Don't swim now, darling. Let's go to bed. Let's make love.'

But apart from the fact that they did not have the apartment to themselves, and she found the presence of Rosie and Theron inhibiting, she was afraid to let him look into her eyes while she lay in his arms, every nerve pulsating in response to that blissful effleurage he had practised on her the night before. It was hard enough never to utter the murmurs of love, the soft words which welled up inside her. But to hide her enraptured expression would be next to impossible. Drogo would know he had conquered her entirely; that he now possessed her heart and soul.

It was a somewhat tense evening. They seemed to have little to say to each other at dinner, and afterwards they watched television, a form of entertainment which she found only moderately interesting, and to which she was certain he had never been addicted.

She felt that a normal bride would have sat close, her head on his shoulder, letting the programmes wash over her, happy just to be near him. But when, after dinner, they had moved from the table to the sofas, Drogo had not seated himself near her, but on one of the two other sofas; and somehow she could not bring herself to move to where he was sitting while his mouth had that slightly grim set and all his attention seemed concentrated on the screen.

That night, in bed, after he had switched off the light,

he did not take her in his arms. But then, in the concealing darkness, Annis had the courage to turn towards him and touch, with tentative fingertips, the warm skin of his chest.

Had he not responded, she would have leaned over and kissed him with one of the kisses he had taught her.

But Drogo did respond—violently. Annis found her head pinned to the pillow a kiss almost cruel in its intensity; and, when his hand was impeded by the lace and satin of her nightdress, with savage impatience he ripped it open.

With a muffled sound of dismay at the needless destruction she braced herself for a swift and brutal possession.

Brutal it was, in a sense, for he still had much more to teach her, and that night he no longer made any allowance for her shyness. Swift it was not. As impatient as he had been at the beginning, now it seemed to please him to prolong her ecstasy. Afterwards she felt exhausted, and knew she would sleep for hours.

The next afternoon she met Matthew Forbes.

He was the curator in charge of a specialised collection of naval and military records housed on the top floor of a tall, narrow house with a creaking, uncarpeted staircase.

The door at the top had a metal plaque bearing the name of the trust which administered the collection, and a cardboard notice *Please Enter*.

Annis knocked before she entered, and found herself in a room with rows of books and labelled box files all round its walls, and a man at a desk in the middle of it.

He was about Drogo's age, but fair and grey-eyed and too thin for his height. Although not as tall as her husband, when he stood up to greet her he showed himself to be above average height, but very lanky.

He appeared to be surprised to see her. 'Good afternoon.

May I help you?' he said in a quiet, pleasant voice.

Annis explained that she was in search of information, and he said, 'I see. This collection is open to the public, but we have some irreplaceable papers here, and it's usual for people who wish to consult it to provide us with some kind of reference. What is the purpose of your research? Is it for a thesis?'

'No, for a biography.'

Again he showed signs of surprise which, smiling slightly, he explained by saying, 'You don't look like an author of books of that nature. Who is your publisher?'

'I haven't one yet—if ever,' Annis admitted. 'The book hasn't been commissioned. I'm doing it for my own pleasure, and hoping it may be good enough to be published when it's finished.'

'I'm afraid you may find the merit of the work is of less importance than its saleability. There used to be an old general who spent many afternoons here, working on a scholarly history of one of the lesser known British garrisons. But although it was a first class work, he couldn't find a publisher for it—the subject was not of sufficiently popular appeal. However I don't want to discourage you, Miss . . .'

'Annis Rossiter.'

She would have corrected this slip of the tongue, but before she could do so, he introduced himself, and said, 'If you haven't a professor or a publisher who can vouch for you, perhaps there is someone else. It may be that a note from your father would be sufficient, if he's a professional man.'

'My father is dead. He was quite a well-known biographer in his day, and my mother wrote history for children under her maiden name. I could get a note from her publisher.

They know me through correspondence.'

In a room adjoining his office a whistling kettle began to boil, and he said, 'Excuse me a moment', and limped towards an inner door to turn it off. Annis couldn't be sure whether his limp was a permanent one or the temporary result of some accident.

Matthew Forbes was absent for two or three minutes, and when he came back, with a tea tray, he said, as he placed it on the desk, 'I'm a fairly good judge of character, and I feel sure you're not the type of person who cuts out colour plates or filches rare books to sell to unscrupulous dealers. If you wish to use our facilities, you may do so, Miss Rossiter. Now before I explain our somewhat eccentric indexes to you, would you care to have a cup of tea?'

'How kind of you. Thank you.'

Again she would have corrected his misapprehension about her name and status, but he went on to ask how she had heard of the collection. By the time she had explained, and he had asked other questions, she had forgotten the matter, and did not think of it again until she was on her way home. Then it seemed to her that, just as her mother had used her maiden name, she would continue to use hers for everything to do with the literary side of her life. Her wedding ring would make it plain to anyone whom it concerned that she was, in fact, a married woman.

All the time she had been in the Quiet Room at the Trust, she had given no thought to her marriage. Browsing through the various indexes and finding her way about the shelves—there had been no one else working there, and Matthew Forbes had withdrawn to the outer room— had, to use an expression she had heard but never fully understood, taken her out of herself.

She found herself looking forward to repeating the experience the next day. It was very absorbing and soothing, this delving into the past. For a time it erased from her mind all the problems and pangs of the present.

'There's a parcel for you from Fortnum and Mason, madam,' said Rosie, when she reached home.

Puzzled, Annis went to her bedroom and opened the box which she found there. Turning back the leaves of tissue paper, she saw an exquisite nightdress of finely pleated peach georgette—clearly an *amende honorable* for Drogo's violence the night before. Obviously he had disposed of the nightdress which this one replaced, as it had disappeared when she had woken that morning.

They had been married for a month when Drogo announced that they were going to revisit Morne Island.

Curious as she was to see her old home, to some extent Annis was reluctant to uproot herself from her new life. By now she was intensely involved in research for her book, greatly aided by Matthew Forbes, who had suggested various sources of information which she might not have discovered unaided.

On the flight across the Atlantic she discovered that Drogo had made a number of arrangements in advance.

Next day, the final lap of the journey back to Morne Island was by a large amphibian helicopter in which they were accompanied by an architect, a surveyor and a man to open up the path to the house.

It was strange to have a bird's eye view of the island. It looked, thought Annis, as they circled above it, like the head of an enormous cauliflower, only rich emerald green instead of creamy-white. From this height the reef appeared as an indigo line between the blue of the ocean and the aquamarine of the sea.

It wasn't until Drogo put his arm round her and gave her his handkerchief that she realised she was seeing it with brimming eyes and a tear trickling down her cheek.

By the time the helicopter had touched down on the glassy water within the protective coral-heads, she had recovered from the sudden upsurge of emotion at the sight of the place which was still 'home' to her.

As they had known it must be, the way to the house had reverted to impenetrable undergrowth which the burly labourer at once set to work to hack through with his machete.

While he was doing this, Drogo suggested that the other three should join him and Annis in a swim, but only the pilot concurred. The architect and his associate preferred to sit in the shade of a palm and refresh themselves with cold beer from one of several cold-boxes brought to sustain the party through the day-long trip.

Because she was wearing a bikini in place of underclothes, it took Annis only seconds to be ready to bathe. As she waded into the warm water, she felt fresh tears sting her eyes—tears of joy at being back in the place she loved best in the world, accompanied by the man she loved, and free now to come and go at will. For her this was heaven on earth; the only flaw being that Drogo did not love her.

But every Eden had its serpent and, compared with most people's lives, she knew that her paradise garden was as near perfection as any human being had a right to expect.

Although she was not yet so blasé—and hoped she never would become so—that swimming in the rooftop pool in London had ceased to be a luxury to her, the artificially heated and chemically treated pool water was not to be compared with this crystal sea with its pale pink coral-sand bed, and its sun-given warmth.

When the sea was up to her waist she threw up her arms and sank into it with almost the same frisson of pleasure as she yielded to Drogo's embrace; and, floating with her eyes closed, every muscle relaxed and the sunlight hot on her face filled her with the same kind of peace as lying in his arms after love.

She swam and played in the water long after the two men had left it. Eventually Drogo came back into the sea and, when he reached her, said, 'I think you should come out now, Annis. You've been in nearly an hour.'

'I could stay in all day. Oh, isn't it glorious!' she exclaimed.

'Yes, it's an idyllic spot and, with some discreet civilisation, will make a splendid holiday place for our offspring, when we have them,' he answered. 'It seems unlikely that anyone who loves the sea as much as you do will have children who aren't enthusiastic water-babies.'

It was his first direct reference to children since before they were married. Presently, standing in the ankle-deep shallows, performing the familiar ritual of twisting her hair into a thick skein and pressing out much of the water, Annis found herself wondering how much the continuing frequency with which Drogo made love was because he desired her for herself. Perhaps, if she knew the truth, her body had long since lost the allure of novelty, and the only reason he still took her in his arms almost every night was because he was a highly-sexed man determined to breed a quiverful as soon as possible.

Perhaps the moment I'm pregnant, he'll start to neglect me, she thought, her exhilaration dying. Especially when my waist goes, and I start looking huge and ungainly. Then he'll probably scarcely come near me, and I'll know he's sleeping with Fiona or, if not her, someone else.

It had not struck her before that she could be pregnant

at this moment; her still-slender body already irreversibly involved in the long, slow process of gestation which, to some men, might give their wives a new kind of beauty, but not, she felt sure, to her husband.

To please him a woman had to be shapely and supple, to walk with a spring in her step, and to have a trim waist and flat stomach. She felt in her bones that Drogo's attitude to women was exactly the same as a sultan's towards his harem. He would take it as his natural right, if she lost her looks for some months, to let her get on with bearing his child while he found pleasure elsewhere.

The prospect made her so miserable that she was afraid it would show in her face. Quickly she put on the loose, gauzy lime green jacket which matched her bikini, and said she would take a can of beer up to Luther, whose machete could still be heard rhythmically slashing and chopping.

'Not in those flimsy sandals, you won't, my girl. Give it to me. I'll take it to him,' said Drogo, putting on his light canvas shoes which offered greater protection on a newly-cut path.

Annis watched him go, slightly cheered by this show of care for her. He might not be faithful for much longer, if indeed he had been up to now, but at least he was considerate and mannerly, which could not be said of all men.

Later, when the way was clear as far as the house, he insisted on carrying her up it to avoid any risk of her stepping on a scorpion or a centipede, or gashing herself on the sharply-shorn remains of a bush.

With her arms round his neck, and his arms under her knees and her back, he mounted the hill to the house shut up for so long.

Annis had known that what had once been the garden

must by now be a wilderness. She was more interested to see what had become of the interior.

When Drogo set her on her feet, she unlocked the door with the heavy, old-fashioned key, but could not open it.

'It's warped, I expect.' He moved her gently aside and put his shoulder to the wood. It gave to the force of his shove, and the hinges creaked as he pushed it wide open.

'Ugh! What a horrible smell!' exclaimed Annis, crossing the threshold.

It was the sour reek of rooms long unaired and unlit. For although they had seldom been closed while she and her father were in residence, the house had glazed windows most of which they had shut before setting out on a trip which they had expected to be of only short duration.

Drogo moved about, opening the windows and shutters, and letting in fresh air and sunshine. It revealed a strange, eerie sight—a room in which every surface was dappled or furred with grey mildew.

The leather-bound books were the worst. Their backstrips thick with the stuff; and her father's red leather chair looked, while the room was half dark, as if it had been re-upholstered with ash-coloured plush.

Seeing her dismay, Drogo said, 'Don't look so appalled. It can soon be set right. Tomorrow I'll send over a team of women to give the place a thorough clean.'

'Oh, no—what a waste of money! I can do it myself,' she objected.

He came to where she was standing, and placed his hands on her shoulders. 'I don't wish you to do it yourself. There are better uses for your time. You'll have to choose all the fittings. I want the place to be finished the next time we come.'

'But the house isn't even designed yet.'

'It will be, before we leave here. I only employ people who are prepared to work flat out to give me what I want—fast. If they can't, they're no use to me.'

She said, without stopping to think, 'And if I don't give you a son in the minimum time, will the same thing apply to me?'

Drogo's expression changed and he looked furious. She would have given a great deal to recall that ill-judged riposte.

His fingers were biting into her shoulders. 'Y-you're hurting me, Drogo,' she stammered.

He said, between clenched teeth, 'There are times when I should like to do more than hurt you, my girl.'

Annis flinched, then recovered herself. 'To strangle me, perhaps? I don't know why you should. It's only the truth, isn't it? We have never made any bones, either of us, about the reasons why we married. You wanted children, and I—I wanted Morne Island.'

'And is it worth it?' he demanded savagely. 'Was today, swimming in the lagoon, worth the price of being my wife last night in bed?'

Hot colour flamed in her cheeks. 'You make it sound as though I only ... put up with you. You know it isn't like that.'

'I know I can give you pleasure. Any man could do that, with the right technique,' he said harshly. 'But when you give yourself to me, it's only your body you surrender, not your mind, not your heart. You don't love me.'

'And you want me to love you, don't you, Drogo? You like mating women who adore you—and then moving on to fresh conquests. Well, you won't ever make *me* your slave. I'm the one women who can resist you.'

She broke into wild, reckless laughter.

'God damn it, I *will* make you love me.' He didn't say it, he snarled it.

'No, you won't. Never—ever. Not ever!' Annis was on the verge of hysteria.

It was at this point that Luther intervened, walking through the front door and saying cheerfully, 'I've had mah lunch break, Mr Wolfe, sir. Is you wishin' for me to clear de garden?'

'Yes, Luther, if you would, please.'

Drogo spoke with meticulous politeness. His hands fell from Annis's shoulders. He turned and walked out of the room, and she heard him opening the windows in the other parts of the house.

For a moment or two she was tempted to rush after him, to blurt out the truth—her love, and her longing for his love. Then her self-control reasserted itself. She gave a long shuddering sigh and walked outside, into the sun.

The paint was peeling from the verandah rail. She picked at the loose faded flakes, remembering some lines from Milton.

But he that hides a dark soul, and foul thoughts,
Benighted walks under the midday sun.

Was it worth it? Drogo had asked her. Was anything worth this torment of unexpressed feeling; this heartbreaking longing to say, I love you. *I love you!*

'I'm sorry, Annis. I lost my temper.'

She had not heard his footsteps behind her, and his quiet apology made her jump.

'I ... I'm sorry, too,' she responded. 'I shouldn't have said what I did. It's only that sometimes——' She left the sentence unfinished.

'Sometimes what?' he prompted.

She shook her head. 'Nothing, really.'

'Sometimes you regret our marriage and wish you'd never set eyes on me—is that it?'

'No—no, never that.' The fervent denial burst from her before she could stop it, just as a short time before she had vehemently denied her love for him. 'H-how could I when you're so good to me?'

'But that's all you feel for me—gratitude?'

'And respect for your mind ... and attraction to your physical presence. Isn't that enough for you, Drogo? Why are you so determined to make me crazy about you? I think it would bore you, if I were.' She kept her tone airy this time, and her eyes on the distant horizon.

He made no comment on this, but she felt he was thinking it over and would, at length, have said something had they not been joined by the architect.

He and the surveyor had been pushing their way through the less dense vegetation of the garden area in order to study the prospect from all points of the compass.

He began to expound his ideas, to which Drogo listened intently and Annis with an appearance of attention. But she found it hard to give her mind to anything but their personal problems.

The next day she spent on her own. Drogo would not allow her to accompany the cleaning women. When she argued about it, he was adamant.

'I don't want you breathing in all that dust. The air will be thick with it when they start brushing the mould off everything. I'll see to it that they don't handle the books too roughly. You can amuse yourself here for one day, I feel sure. If you get bored with the beach, go shopping in town.'

As he said this, they were having breakfast on the verandah of their cottage, one of a complex of holiday cottages in the beautifully landscaped grounds of a mansion which had been converted into a country club.

Beyond the verandah was a lawn, and beyond that a mile-long beach of castor sugar sand shaded, here and there, by grass-thatched sun shelters and set about with cushioned loungers. On these, later, in the morning, the occupants of the other cottages would stretch out and sip cooling drinks brought to them by Lyall, the steward in charge of the thatched beach bar.

This side of Caribbean life was one which Annis had glimpsed but never experienced. Certainly it was no hardship to be left on her own in such surroundings and, had she wished, she could easily have made the acquaintance of some of the other people staying there.

However she preferred to keep to herself, alternately swimming and reading—or rather giving the appearance of reading although, in reality, she was only gazing blindly at the pages, her mind on the man who, did he but know it, had long since succeeded in his determination to make her love him.

Later, as he had suggested, she went to look at the shops, not intending to buy but succumbing to a dress of ocean-coloured chiffon with a scatter of beads on the under-layer of the skirt, and beaded and sequinned shoulder straps. Already, after only three days back in the sun—for Drogo had insisted on a rest day following the long flight from London—her skin was beginning to recover its honey-gold sheen.

It was dark before he returned and, having put on the new dress because he had said they would dine and dance at the big house, she was thinking of taking it off in case he was tired and preferred to eat at the cottage. Not that she had ever known him to evince any signs of fatigue. His energy seemed inexhaustible.

Before she had made up her mind, she was distracted by the radio and the opening bars of one of her favourite tunes, *Feelings*, played by a clarinet with strings in the background. The tender melody with its undertones of sadness had touched her heart long before Drogo had given her permanent heartache. Now, combined with the visual beauty of the silver sea and lantern-lit gardens, and her present emotional sensitivity, it moved her even more deeply.

In the middle of it Drogo came round the corner and found her standing on the verandah with the night breeze fluttering her skirt and tears sparkling on her lashes.

If he saw them, he made no remark but said crisply, 'Sorry I'm late, but it won't take me long to shower and change.'

He went straight to the bathroom, and Annis switched off the music and quickly pulled herself together.

She was in the bedroom when he emerged from the bathroom, a towel bound round his lean hips.

She said, 'If you've had a tiring day, I'm quite content to have supper here.'

'Tiring? No, not at all tiring. I did very little, apart from keeping an eye on the women who tackled the bookshelves. You'll be glad to hear they seem in better condition than one might have expected. Tomorrow you can decide which you want to have shipped back to England and which can remain where they are. What have you been doing with yourself?'

She told him. 'I bought this dress. Do you like it?' She stood up to show him the line of it.

He gave it a glance, but it was not the critical scrutiny

he usually gave whenever she canvassed his opinion. Perhaps he had the house on his mind, as the next thing he said was, 'Have a look at the roughs which the architect has drawn up.'

He indicated a plastic folder he had thrown on his side of the bed, and went back to the bathroom where Annis heard him using his electric razor.

Annis opened the folder and was surprised to find in it various colour photographs of the island, including some aerial shots, mounted on the first pages. Then there were visualisations of the same house in different positions, including one where it was cantilevered out over a steep bluff. Finally there were the ground plans.

'Can you make sense of those?' Drogo asked, coming back to dress. 'Not everyone can read a plan.'

'I find these quite clear,' she said, studying the different layouts, all of them permutations of the same amount of accommodation. 'Have you had time to look at them yet?'

'No, I only picked them up on the way through town. I'll study them in the morning. At the moment, my mind is on dinner.'

But although he had said this, Annis noticed that he took less than his usual interest in the restaurant's extensive menu of Caribbean specialities, and when the food came he toyed with it, which was not at all like him.

Eventually she said, 'Drogo, are you feeling all right? You seem to have very little appetite tonight.'

'I'm fine ... merely not very hungry.'

'But that's so unlike you. Are you *sure* you're not unwell?'

'Perfectly sure. You haven't lived with me long enough to know that I often go off my food when I'm hatching a project or working out a problem.'

'I shouldn't have thought the house was a sufficiently major project to affect you in that way.'

'It isn't,' he agreed.

'Then it must be a problem. Is it one you can talk about to me? Or would it be over my head?'—assuming that it must be something to do with his business empire.

'You are my problem, Annis,' he told her.

'I am? What do you mean?'

'We can't discuss it here. Let's go for a walk on the beach.'

As they left the restaurant by a door giving directly on to the garden, Annis felt prickles of apprehension running along her nerves. There had been something ominous in his tone. She realised now that, all evening, his mood had been subtly different from any of his previous attitudes.

'Drogo, don't keep me in suspense. Why am I suddenly a problem?' she asked anxiously, while they were still on the path which wound its way through the luxuriant shrubberies of poinciana, hibiscus and bougainvillea.

'Because you're the only person who, in my adult life, I haven't been able to bend to my will,' he replied. 'For about fifteen years I've been accustomed to having everyone around me dance to my tune—except you.' He paused for a moment before continuing, 'Now I realise it was unfair to pressure you into marriage, believing that you were sufficiently young and malleable to become what I wanted you to become. Your outburst yesterday, at the house, made me see that you have more steel in your character than I'd foreseen.'

They had come to the edge of the gardens where they marched with the beach, and where a low wall kept back the sand and provided a perch for Annis to unfasten her high-heeled sandals. Before she could bend to deal with them, Drogo went down on his haunches to undo the buckles for her.

'Surely you wouldn't want me to be completely spineless?' she said uncertainly. She was not sure where this was leading.

He said, 'Nor do I want you to be unhappy which, clearly, you are. You'd been crying when I came in tonight.'

He slipped the sandals off her feet and, holding them by the heel-straps, stood up.

'Not really crying,' she protested. 'I expect it sounds foolish to you, but certain music can make me feel sad. That was all it was, Drogo—the music. Nothing to do with us.'

'Nothing?' He put his hand under her chin and tilted her face to the moonlight. 'Is that the truth, Annis ... the whole truth?'

Her innate honesty made her hesitate, causing him to say crisply, 'No, of course it's not the whole truth. You aren't happy, but by now it may be too late to cut our losses.'

'Cut our losses?—I don't understand you.'

They were walking over the sand now. It was warm beneath her bare feet.

'Within a few hours of our wedding, you wanted me to release you. I wouldn't listen to you then. I dismissed it as bridal jitters. Now it may be that we have not only ourselves to consider. You could very easily be pregnant, and to me it's a rule of life that a child has a right to two parents, if both are alive and responsible for their actions.'

'You mean ... if you could be sure that I'm not pregnant, you would send me away?' Annis asked tensely.

'Not send you away—release you.'

'But I don't want to be released now. Unless you're

already tired of me. Is that what you really mean, Drogo?'

He laid a hard hand on her shoulder and swung her to face him. 'Certainly not. As far as I'm concerned nothing has changed. But I'm not such a brute that I want to hold you under duress.'

She wasn't sure how to answer him. She could never forget his own dictum—Never let a man know you're hooked until you know he's hooked by you.

With a gesture which embraced the moon-silvered sea, the pale beach and the golden lights of the hinterland, she said, 'If this is duress, I'm sure there are millions of women who would be very happy to change places with me, Drogo.'

He looked at her for a long time, his face in shadow, unreadable. At last he said, 'I think I still have a problem. But maybe time will solve it. Meanwhile——'

He swung her, unresisting, into his arms, and began to walk back to the cottage.

Annis had always supposed that where there was no love there could be no jealousy. That it could be activated merely by possessiveness was brought home to her the afternoon several weeks later, when Matthew Forbes told her about his private life. He revealed that he was a widower with an eight-year-old daughter in the care of his mother. His wife had been dead several years, killed in the car accident which had left him with a game leg. The crash had not been his fault but that of another motorist, but he still blamed himself for not making his wife wear the seat belt which might have reduced her injuries.

He confided to Annis his worry that his mother's failing health would not allow her to keep house for him much longer. Then who would look after his daughter during the difficult transition from childhood to adolescence?

'The fact is I've fallen in love, but with someone years younger than me. Would any girl of, say, twenty, want to lumber herself with a man with a limp and a ready-made daughter of eight?' he asked gloomily.

'If she loved you—yes, of course she would.'

He brooded on this for some minutes. Then he said, 'The girl is you, Annis. I fell in love with you the first time you walked into this office. I didn't believe it could happen. But it did; and all our conversations since then have confirmed that you really are as gentle, and kind, and sympathetic as you looked to be, that first day.'

He reached out to take her hands, and she was too stunned to withdraw them, and sat staring at him incredulously.

It was at this difficult juncture that Drogo, who was not due back from Lille until late in the evening, walked into the office and saw Matthew kissing her hands.

'What the hell is going on here?' he demanded, as instinctively Annis snatched her hands out of the other man's clasp.

Matthew looked both startled and discomfited. 'Do you know this man?'

'She should. She's been sleeping with me for some time.' Drogo's eyes were brilliant with anger. She had never seen him look more dangerous.

For a moment Matthew was stupefied. Then he turned to her for confirmation.

'This is Drogo Wolfe ... my husband,' she told him. 'Drogo, this is Matthew Forbes, the curator here. Please don't lose your temper,' she added hurriedly.

Neither man acknowledged the introduction. Matthew said, 'But I had no idea you were married. You told me your surname was Rossiter. And you look too young ... too ...'

Before he had found the word he wanted, she said, 'I wear a wedding ring, Matthew. My mother used her maiden name for her work. It's not an uncommon practice.'

'I can see you do now,' he said, looking at her rings. 'But I'm afraid I'm not very observant over clothes and jewellery. I was going by your ...' Again he floundered for words to explain what had made him take it for granted that she was single.

Annis turned to her husband. 'How is it you're back so much earlier than you expected?'

'Let it suffice that I am,' he said curtly. 'As Rosie said you spent much of your time working here, I came to see what the place has to offer. Get your things. I'm taking you home.'

Annis opened her mouth to object, thought better of it, and went to collect her bag and her papers from the Quiet Room.

When she returned to the outer office Drogo said, 'Make sure you haven't forgotten anything, because you won't be coming back.'

Again she forced herself to bite back a furious retort.

'Goodbye, Matthew. I'm sorry I didn't make my position plainer. It just didn't seem necessary.'

'I'm sorry, too,' he said awkwardly. 'Goodbye, Annis.'

Neither she nor her husband spoke on their way down the stairs. In the street outside he grasped her elbow and hailed a taxi.

'Aren't you jumping to some rather hasty conclusions?' she said, as the cab moved off.

'Am I? Then explain them away.'

'Had you come a few minutes earlier, there would have been nothing to explain.'

She recounted what Matthew had told her about his domestic circumstances.

'I was flabbergasted when he seemed to think I might be a suitable substitute mother for his daughter. You'll just have to take my word for it that he never touched me, or said anything of a personal nature to me, until this afternoon—immediately before your arrival.'

To her surprise Drogo said, much more amiably, 'Very well, I'll take your word for it.' He reached out his arm and drew her to him. 'Which is more than you did in similar circumstances,' he said dryly, before his mouth claimed hers in a kiss which drove all other thoughts from her mind.

Drogo's next trip was to New York, and although he was going for a week he said he would be too busy to make it worthwhile for her to accompany him. In his absence Annis went to a fashion show, in aid of charity, at one of London's famous stores.

Most of the other women there seemed to be with a friend, but she was not the only person to have come on her own. Soon after she had sat down, the chair next to hers was taken by a rather tall woman in green who gave Annis a friendly smile as she seated herself. Presently she made a remark about the banks of flowers along the sides of the catwalk, and this led them into a conversation which continued until the chairs immediately behind theirs were taken. A few moments later a voice said, 'Good afternoon, Mrs Wolfe.'

Annis turned. She found herself looking at a woman to whom she had been introduced at a recent dinner party, but with whom she had had practically no conversation and whose name she couldn't recall.

'Oh ... hello,' she said, with a smile, hoping her lapse of memory was not apparent.

The woman's glance shifted to Annis's neighbour, who now was studying her programme.

The woman behind said, 'Hello, my dear. How are you? I didn't know you two knew each other.'

With obvious reluctance, the woman in green turned her head and said, 'Good afternoon, Millicent. Mrs Wolfe and I haven't met, but I'm sure you'll be delighted to introduce us.'

Her tone held a distinct note of sarcasm which puzzled Annis until her dinner-party acquaintance answered, with saccharine sweetness, 'I'd be delighted. What a small world it is, isn't it? Mrs Wolfe, this is Mrs Riversley ... Fiona Riversley, a very old friend of your husband's. How strange that you've never met each other until today.'

CHAPTER SIX

ANNIS felt herself turning pale. Although, since returning from Paris, she had tried her best never to let her mind dwell on the woman with whom Drogo had spent part of the night before their mariage, she had never been able entirely to forget her existence. It was a considerable shock to find that this pleasant-seeming person to whom she had been making small-talk was the one who had wrecked her wedding day.

For that this Fiona and that Fiona were one and the same was made obvious not only by the catty enjoyment with which the woman behind them had performed the introduction, but also by Mrs Riversley's own manner.

She's admitted that she knew who I was. She must have recognised me from the wedding photographs in the newspapers, thought Annis. Why did she sit down next to me? There were other chairs she could have taken. She sat next to me and started a conversation deliberately.

Aloud, she said, 'How do you do?'

Then the commère appeared on the dais at one end of the catwalk, and the buzz of chatter subsided as she began her introduction.

Afterwards Annis could remember little of the show, except that it seemed to go on for ever and while everyone else was concentrating on the models as they strode back and forth, she was wondering if it would have showed greater self-possession to have murmured something to the effect that Drogo had mentioned Mrs Riversley to her.

Perhaps not: the less said the better. And one thing was certain; whatever she had said or not said, the woman behind her would be sure to recount the incident to all her cronies.

My dears, would you believe who were sitting side by side at the dress show the other day? Drogo's bride and his erstwhile popsie? Or maybe erstwhile is not the operative word. The bride has heard rumours, clearly. She went quite green, poor little thing ...

Immediately the show ended, she rose and with a coolly courteous word of farewell to each of the two other women, made her way to the lifts and thence to one of the side doors.

In the street she paused for a moment. Usually she walked everywhere, but it looked as if it might rain so perhaps it would be wiser to hail a taxi before the shower started and any taxis with lighted For Hire signs became non-existent.

Or she could hole up in a café and drink tea until the rain cleared. If she went home, and Rosie was in, she would insist on making the tea, and Annis was not in the mood to be waited on by anyone but a waitress who would be too busy to pay more than the most cursory attention to her.

As she stood on the pavement, undecided, there was a light touch on her arm and she turned to find Fiona Riversley standing beside her.

'Mrs Wolfe, forgive me, but I must talk to you ... apologise ...'

'Apologise?' Annis said blankly.

'Knowing who you were, I shouldn't have sat next to you and given that wretched woman the chance to make mischief. It was obvious, when she introduced us, that you were very upset by learning who I was. You didn't let Millicent see it, but I couldn't help noticing how tightly your hands were clenched all through the show, and I guessed that someone—an even bigger bitch than Millicent—had told you that your husband and I were once the subject of a good deal of gossip among the scandal-mongers.'

'Once, Mrs Riversley?' Annis tried to make her tone cutting.

But strangely the jealous dislike she had felt for the un-known Fiona did not pierce her as sharply now that she had the flesh and blood woman standing beside her under the canopy of the store's doorway.

Had she been of the same type as Millicent—a woman no longer young but made up like an over-painted girl, with hard eyes and a sulky mouth—Annis could have hated her. But Mrs Riversley was not like that.

Now, seen face to face, she confirmed the impression she had given during their conversation before the show; that she was an intelligent, outgoing person in her forties whose blonde-streaked brown hair might owe its colour to the skill of her hairdresser, but whose make-up was so light and subtle that it made no attempt to camouflage the lines round her eyes, but merely gave the impression of a woman, once beautiful, on sensible terms with the inevitable changes of growing older, and still extremely attractive. There was warmth and kindness in the blue eyes looking at Annis, and good humour in the lines of her lips. Millicent, who also had blue eyes, had been wear-ing blue which had made them seem pale. Mrs Riversley's green linen suit made her eyes a deep blue.

'Yes, a long time ago—certainly long before you came into his life,' was her answer to Annis's interrogative com-ment.

'The last time I heard the story was on my wedding

day,' said Annis. 'And it wasn't referred to in the past tense.'

'What!' The older woman looked appalled. 'Oh, surely not?' she exclaimed distressfully. 'I can hardly believe that anyone could be so vile as to gossip to *you* on your wedding day. And yet I know from experience that people can be unutterably vile,' she added, in a low voice. 'They pass on and even embroider tales with hardly any foundation.'

'This gossip had some foundation. Drogo *had* been to see you, late the night before our marriage.'

'And someone saw him, and implied that—oh, my God! How shameful—how wicked! If only they knew the real reason ...' Her voice broke, her eyes filled with tears.

It was at this moment that a taxi swung in close to the kerb, and a man jumped out and stood by the nearside front window to pay the driver.

'We must talk, and we can't here,' said Mrs Riversley, urging Annis into the back of the cab.

To the driver, when he slid aside the glass partition and asked, 'Where to, lady?' she said, 'Just drive round the Park for ten minutes, would you, please?'

Then, to Annis, 'I'm sorry, I'm not usually so emotional, but even to think of that night ... If I hadn't had Drogo to turn to ... but of course he told you all about it.'

'No ... no, he didn't. Only that the reason need not concern me.'

'Well, no, it didn't; but I should have thought he would have told you, especially after you heard about it at second-hand—the whole thing completely distorted and as far from the truth as the Poles.'

Annis said nothing. It was clear to her now that, unless Mrs Riversley was a remarkably good actress, her reactions were not only genuine but implied a very different set of circumstances from those which had lain, like lead weights, in the depths of her consciousness since the day of her marriage.

'Although Drogo gave me his word—as if I needed it— that no one else would ever hear from his lips what happened at my flat that night, it never occurred to me his silence would include you,' Fiona Riversley went on. 'He must have exceptional confidence in your trust in him.'

'Yes, but it was misplaced confidence,' said Annis, with shame in her voice. 'I—I couldn't help wondering at times if . . . if perhaps . . . if it had been a farewell visit to you.'

'Our farewell was said long before that ghastly night,' said Fiona. 'Perhaps it's as well that you and I have met like this. No wonder you looked so upset! I thought you were furious with me for having had the gall to indulge my curiosity by speaking to you. But it was always on the cards that our social lives would overlap sooner or later, and when I saw you today I couldn't resist a few words with the girl who had wrought such a change in a man I once thought was heartless.'

She stretched out her hand to touch Annis's arm for a moment. 'Don't misunderstand me. When I was one of the many women who passed in and out of his life before he met you, and loved you, I never knew him to be anything but kind and generous in his private life. I used the word "heartless" in the sense of lacking the capacity to fall deeply in love. Not all men are capable of it. In fact, rather few, I suspect. Most women could give a man their lifelong devotion, if they found out who was worthy of it. But, in general, men who are still unmarried at thirty, and have had many casual relationships, are not likely to spend the last forty years of their life-span in contented fidelity to one woman. However, after what he said to me that night, I believe he is an exception to the rule that there's no such thing as a reformed rake.'

There was a slight catch in her voice as she added, 'Lucky you! To be loved like that by a man like Drogo must be unimaginably wonderful.'

'What was it he told you that night?' Annis asked, on a tense, indrawn breath.

'When it was all over—the crisis which had forced me to turn to him, and which I'll explain in a moment—I wished him happiness with you. He looked at me with a very strange expression in his eyes, and he said, "If I can make her love me as much as I love her, I shall be happier than I've ever expected or deserved to be." I thought it was a curious remark, particularly when I saw the photographs of your wedding in which you were looking up at him with your whole face lit up with love. But I suppose he thought that, because you were very much younger, it would take time for your emotions to reach maturity.'

Annis looked at her long and thoughtfully. 'Did you ... do you love Drogo?' she asked.

Mrs Riversley took a moment or two to answer, 'No. I was flattered by his interest in me. It was marvellous for my morale. But we were merely two people who, having no satisfactory permanent relationship, enjoyed each other's company for a short time. As you may have been told, I'm separated from my second husband, which tends to make people who don't know the full circumstances think I must be a voracious man-eater.'

'No, I didn't know that.'

'In fact, my first marriage was very successful,' Fiona continued. 'I'm sure it would have lasted had my husband not died in his twenties, leaving me with two babies, no insurance and no career. I married again largely to give them security and a good education. But my second husband is a man in whom ambition amounts to an incurable disease. He wanted a hostess, not a wife. I was bored by public life, and he was bored by domestic life. When my two sons, and his three children, were in their late teens, we agreed to go our separate ways. It was one of his daughters who forced my hand the night before your wedding. Believe me, I wouldn't have appealed to Drogo for help if there'd been anyone else who could have handled the situation.'

'What happened?' asked Annis.

'My two elder stepchildren are dears. I'm as fond of them as of my own two. But the younger girl has always been a problem. Perhaps losing her real mother, and resenting my advent, started it. Perhaps she was born a mixed-up personality. Anyway, that night she and a young man—a drop-out—invaded my flat, and behaved in a way which really frightened me. I thought they were both "high" on drugs, and capable of anything. I daren't ring the police because of the risk of publicity and the damage to my husband's career if it came out that one of his children was a hippie.'

'Why didn't you call him to deal with her?'

'Because, as ill-luck would have it, he was out of England on a fact-finding tour. So I locked myself in my bedroom, and rang the one man I knew who would never be floored by any emergency. He came at once, with his manservant who restrained my stepdaughter from interfering while Drogo handled her boy-friend. I don't know how he bundled him out of the building without attracting attention, but he did. Then he came back and dealt with my stepdaughter while Theron was tidying up the mess they'd made. Afterwards, when she'd been taken away to a private clinic where she's still under treatment, Drogo stayed until I had calmed down and was fit to be left on my own. He rang me the next night from Paris, to make sure I was all right, and once more from London a fortnight later. I haven't heard from him since, and shouldn't expect to. He proved a true friend in trouble, and not many people are that when it comes to the crunch.'

'It was lucky he was at home that evening,' said Annis.

'Yes, incredibly lucky. I don't like to think how it might have ended had he not been. So you see, any slight misgivings which you may have had about him and me were entirely unfounded. I'm part of his past, but not of his present and future. They are your domain,' said Fiona, leaning forward to tap on the glass. 'Do you want to be taken home now?'

Annis looked to see where they were, and noticed the clouds had passed over and, with them, the threat of a downpour.

'No, if he'll drop me here, I'll walk the rest of the way.'

She would have paid some of the fare, but Fiona would not allow it.

'Shall you tell Drogo we've met? I rather hope not,' she admitted. 'I should hate him to feel annoyed with me when I'm so much in his debt.'

'I don't know,' Annis said candidly. 'I think I might have to. I would always prefer to be straight with him. But it could have been sheer coincidence that caused our meeting, Mrs Riversley. I don't have to say there were other seats you could have taken.'

The tall, slender woman in green, who had turned out to be so unlike Annis's idea of her, gave her a warm smile.

'Goodbye, Mrs Wolfe—and good luck. I can see why Drogo fell in love with you.'

And then she climbed back in the cab, and waved her hand once before it sped her away.

Annis walked home on air, thinking—He loves me. Drogo loves me.

But if he loved her, why had he never said so?

As soon as she reached the apartment, she put through a call to his hotel, forgetting that late afternoon in London was noon in New York, and he was unlikely to be there at that time of day. The switchboard operator promised to have the message that she had called him left in his suite.

From eleven o'clock until midnight, she lay in bed reading and hoping there might be a call from her husband who by now should be back at the hotel, changing to go out to dinner.

She had fallen asleep with the light on when at last the telephone rang. She heard an American voice saying, 'You're through to London, Mr Wolfe,' and then Drogo's distinctive, deep voice, 'Annis? I'm sorry to wake you, but I've only just come in and found your message waiting for me. Is anything wrong? Why did you call?'

She sat up in bed wide awake, although it was now half past five, and half past midnight where he was.

'Nothing's wrong. How is your trip going?'

'Satisfactorily. Why did you call?'

'To tell you I miss you. To ask if there was any possibility of your coming home sooner than you planned.'

There was silence at the other end of the line.

'Perhaps. I'm not sure. I could try.'

Before her encounter with Fiona, Annis would have taken his tone to indicate reluctance. Now her enlightened ear detected only the cautious response of a man unaccustomed to the idea that his bride could be lonely for him.

'I should have gone with you,' she said. 'I didn't realise

a few days could seem like weeks, or how large a double bed is when there's only one person in it.'

There was another long pause.

At length, Drogo said, 'I may be able to cut some of my appointments.'

'Oh, don't, if it's very inconvenient. I daresay I shall survive without you till Saturday. But it will be lovely to have you back.'

She was really burning her boats now. She could only have made it plainer by saying, *Darling Drogo, I love you desperately*. But that irrevocable admission she would save till she was in his arms.

'I'll see what can be done. You'd better go back to sleep now, and I must get some rest, too. Goodnight, Annis. Thank you for calling.'

The words were unemotional, even formal. But it seemed to her that she could hear an undertone of strong emotion in his voice.

'Goodnight . . . darling.'

Perhaps the last word came too late for him to catch it before he put down his receiver and cut the connection.

But it didn't matter if he hadn't heard it. She had the rest of her life to speak the soft words of love to him.

Leaning over to replace the receiver and switch out the light, she then snuggled down under the clothes, and lay counting the hours to his return and the true beginning of their life together.

She did not expect him to call her again much before noon the next day. But when the afternoon passed with no call from Drogo to say he had re-thought his schedule and either could or could not fly home a day or two earlier, she began to fidget and worry.

She had lived too long under a dark cloud of insecurity for her new-found confidence in the future to be invulnerable to fresh doubts.

She was alone in the flat that day, Rosie and Theron having left early to visit some friends now in business on the south coast. They were not coming back until late. So it was with surprise that, while she was in the kitchen, making herself a light supper of devilled scrambled eggs, as she often had in her bedsitter days, that she heard the signal that the lift was ascending to the top floor.

Concluding that they had come back early for some reason, she went on beating the ingredients while the butter heated in the pan.

When a voice called out, 'Where are you, Annis?' she was so amazed and excited that she almost forgot to draw the pan off the heat before rushing to answer that unmistakable voice.

'Drogo! How did you get here so quickly?'

'On Concorde. You haven't changed your mind and decided you like being a grass widow, have you?'

'No ... no, I've spent all afternoon wondering why you hadn't been in touch. It never even crossed my mind that you might be on your way back. What a glorious surprise—but what about the rest of your engagements?'

'To hell with them,' he said dismissively. 'They can wait, but I couldn't after talking to you last night. Come here.'

He held out his arms to her and, with shining eyes, she flew into a crushing embrace.

They kissed until she was breathless. When at last Drogo raised his head, he said huskily, 'I should have gone away sooner if I'd thought that a few days' absence would result in this warm welcome back. The old saying must be true:

absence does make the heart grow fonder.'

Her face hidden against his shoulder, she said, 'The heart has always been fond, but I never dared to admit it because you once told me a girl should never let a man know that she loves him before he's told her he loves her.'

She leaned backwards in his strong arms and looked up into his face. 'I thought at the time it was good advice—especially with someone like you. But now I think it's very bad advice. Love shouldn't make cowards of people; it should make them brave and generous. I haven't been either, but I mean to be from now on. I love you, Drogo. I love you so much that I don't even care if, later, you have other women. As long as I'm——'

'Don't say that,' he interrupted. 'There'll never be any other women now I have you. Do you take me for one of those men who need a succession of extra-marital adventures to bolster their egos? I'm not. Since I was in my early twenties, I've wanted one woman, and one woman only. The difficulty was to find one who would fulfil all my needs.'

'Do I? Can I?' she whispered.

'Yes ... yes ... *yes*!' he said fiercely, straining her close to his heart again. 'You can give me everything, Annis. All I need, for the rest of my life—if you love me as much as I love you.'

'Why did you never tell me before?—That you loved me.'

'I hoped that whenever, if ever, I succeeded in making you love me, you would recognise my love for you from my actions rather than my words. Like you, I was a coward—afraid to confide what I felt to a girl whom I'd badgered into marriage. But when you told me you'd missed me, your voice wasn't cool any more, and I had to come home to find out if your eyes matched your voice.'

'And do they?' she asked, with a melting smile.

Drogo didn't answer, but swept her up into his arms, and carried her through to their bedroom where they made love and, for the first time, she was not ashamed of his power to command her reactions.

'Darling ... darling ...' she murmured exultantly, no longer fearing the light which now revealed not only her ecstatic surrender, but the tenderness mixed with his passion.

How could she ever have doubted that he loved her? she wondered afterwards, lying at peace, his cheek against hers, their bodies still fused by the fire which had kindled between them.

I should have known that he loved me when he always stayed in my arms, she thought dreamily. Why did I ever need words when almost his every action was a clear sign of how he felt?

'Am I crushing you, sweet?' Drogo murmured.

'No, I like it. Why don't you sleep? You must be tired, aren't you?' she said, trying to make him relax.

In spite of his question, the weight of his tall, powerful frame was not resting on her slender form but on his own elbows.

'It's flying west which is tiring. Admittedly I didn't sleep too soundly last night, after we'd talked. But I had a long nap on the plane. Which reminds me, I have something for you.'

With a light kiss, he moved away and swung off the bed.

'You needn't have put that on. Rosie and Theron are out until quite late tonight, and I shall be cooking your supper,' said Annis when, in his dark red silk dressing-gown, Drogo came back from the sitting-room with his suitcase and briefcase.

From the latter he took a flat parcel, then returned to the bed.

Hoistering herself into a sitting position, now as unselfconscious about her nakedness as before she had always been shy of him seeing her undressed, she asked, 'A present from New York?'

'No, from London,' he said, as he piled up the pillows behind her. 'Actually I chose it for you some time ago, but the shop had only just bought it from the previous owner, and it needed cleaning, and also to have a case made for it. I had a card to advise me it was ready on the morning I left for New York, and I stopped off to collect it for you on my way back from the airport. I hope you'll like it, my lovely.'

He tore off the thick wrapping paper, revealing a shagreen case which, when he opened it, contained something which made her gasp.

She had a brief glimpse of the whole before Drogo lifted the necklace from its velvet bed and fastened it round her slim neck so that the magnificent pendant of diamonds and rubies hung between her bare ivory breasts. The chain was ornate, of red gold also sprinkled with diamonds.

'It wasn't made as a necklace,' he told her. 'It's a *ferronière*. I'm told the name comes from a portrait by Leonardo in the Louvre. It's called *La Belle Ferronière*, and the subject was once thought to be the beautiful wife of a blacksmith who was loved by François the First. She has a black cord round her head holding a diamond on her forehead, and this set the fashion in England for similar ornaments in the first few years of the Victorian reign when there was a great vogue for jewellery in the style of the Middle Ages.'

'It's ravishing, Drogo!' she exclaimed, looking down at the glowing rubies and glittering diamonds.

He was sitting on the side of the bed, and she held out her arms to draw his head to her and thank him with a gentle kiss.

'Whatever you wear it with, it will never look better than it does at this moment,' he said, when at length she reclined on her pillows once more.

He could still make her blush when that certain glint lit his eyes, but it was no longer a blush of girlish discomfiture but that of a woman basking in the caressing scrutiny of a lover to whom she is not yet fully accustomed.

'Bring me a mirror, would you, darling?'

As he went to fetch one from her dressing-table, her eyes were caught by the gold lettering stamped on the dark green satin lining of the lid of the box.

It was the name of the jewellers whom he had intended to visit on the morning after their wedding, and from whom she had suspected him of buying a present for Fiona.

'You say you chose this some time ago. Before we were married?' she asked him.

'No, afterwards—the day afterwards, to be precise. I thought a jewel might be a small compensation for the loss of your treasured virginity, but they hadn't anything suitable except that.'

He gave her the mirror, and Annis looked at her reflection.

'I couldn't look less virginal at the moment,' she said, seeing her tumbled hair, the heaviness of her eyelids, her lips and the tips of her breasts made tumid by passionate kisses. 'Would you have married me if I'd had other lovers?'

'If you'd had only one, perhaps. I'm not sure. I see the irrationality of a double standard, but still it pleases me to know that no other man has seen you as you look now.

It's curious how jewels make a naked woman doubly erotic. You look like a Caucasian odalisque.'

Annis put the mirror aside. With one sudden supple movement she lay with her head on his thigh and her eyes smiling up into his with a sparkle of laughter.

'Will you buy me a ruby for my navel?'

Drogo's lean dark cheeks creased with amusement.

'Anything ... anything you want.'

He stroked a roundabout course from her throat to her thighs, his expression gradually changing from a smile to an oddly stern look.

'What a fool I was not to realise we could have reached this stage much sooner. I, who thought I knew all about women, but didn't know my wife loved me. It was folly— I see that now—to expect you to take my word that you had no cause to be jealous of my visit to Fiona Riversley's flat.'

Should she tell him she knew that now? Annis wondered uncertainly.

He went on, 'But knowing how even the nicest women find it hard to keep something a secret, I made Theron, who was there with me, say he wouldn't confide in his wife, and I felt it would be a mistake for me to explain it to you. The fact is, I suppose, I was riled by your demand for an explanation. But anyone who can conceal her true feelings as completely as you have from me is capable of keeping a confidence to herself, so I'll tell you now what made me go there that night, of all nights.'

She put her fingertips against his lips. 'No, Drogo— it isn't necessary. I already know why you went, and it makes me love you all the more for your loyalty to a friend in trouble, and feel more ashamed of not trusting you as I do now, and always shall in future.'

'How do you know why I went?' he asked, frowning.

Annis sat up and explained, merely omitting to mention that Mrs Riversley could have sat elsewhere, and had spoken to her before being introduced by the woman called Millicent.

'So now there are no more barriers to our understanding of each other. You have my heart and I, unbelievably, have yours,' she said happily.

As she spoke she slipped one hand inside the red silk of his robe and placed it over his heart. 'You feel as warm and as solid as a rock which has had the sun on it.'

His serious look lightened. Smiling, he copied her gesture.

'And you feel as soft as a dove.'

'You can't feel my heart beating there.'

'No, but I can feel mine.'

So could she. Suddenly, against her palm she could feel the throbbing of a strong, accelerated heartbeat as his ardour revived and ignited the flame in his eyes.

As she swayed towards him, her breathing quickening, it flashed through her mind that perhaps on this first day of marriage as marriage should be, they might make the first of his sons. And before the pressure of his mouth made thinking impossible, she knew that neither her work on the biography, nor retaining possession of the island, nor being the wife of a man who could adorn her like a queen, had an iota of importance compared with the joy of giving Drogo what *he* wanted.

Harlequin Plus
A FAMOUS GREEK MYTH

Annis's father, Sylvanus, spent fifteen years on his "voluminous retelling" of Greek myths. No doubt he included the one about Persephone (pronounced per-sef-a-nee), for this particular legend explains why season follows season and why the earth blossoms and dies and blossoms once again.

Persephone was the maiden of spring, the daughter of the goddess Demeter who ruled the harvest. Between them they bestowed on the earth the gifts of the fields.

But Hades, god of the underworld, fell in love with Persephone. One day as Persephone was playing in the meadows of Sicily, he rose up through a chasm in the earth and carried her off to his kingdom.

Demeter heard her daughter's cries, and she descended from Mount Olympus, the home of the gods, to wander the earth in search of her beloved child. She assumed the appearance of a tired old woman, and the land became barren.

Zeus, the supreme deity, realized that powerful Hades must give way. He dispatched Hermes, his winged messenger, to the underworld. When Hermes arrived with his message from Zeus, Persephone begged Hades to release her. Hades loved her dearly and agreed to send her home if she promised to return to him for five months of each year.

When Demeter saw her daughter the earth became green and fertile again. Then, after seven months had passed, Persephone remembered her promise and returned to Hades to help him rule the kingdom of the dead.

Every year, in fact, Persephone remembers her promise. And it is during her five months with Hades that her mother becomes old again, and all growing things sleep until the maiden of spring comes back to earth.